HE-MAN

AND THE MASTERS OF THE UNIVERSE™

TALES OF ETERNIA

BOOK 1

THE HUNT FOR MOSS MAN

BY GREGORY MONE

AMULET BOOKS • NEW YORK

Library of Congress Control Number 2022932329

ISBN 978-1-4197-5449-4

MASTERS OF THE UNIVERSE™ and associated trademarks and trade dress are owned by, and used under license from, Mattel. © 2022 Mattel.

Edited by Howard W. Reeves

Book design by Deena Fleming

Printed and bound in U.S.A.
10 9 8 7 6 5 4 3 2 1

Amulet Books are available at special discounts when purchased in quantity for premiums and promotions as well as fundraising or educational use. Special editions can also be created to specification. For details, contact specialsales@abramsbooks.com or the address below.

Amulet Books® is a registered trademark of Harry N. Abrams, Inc.

ABRAMS The Art of Books
195 Broadway, New York, NY 10007
abramsbooks.com

TO MO, FOR TOO MANY TOYS

AN EVIL POWER

rules over the planet Eternia. The brother of King Randor has transformed himself into the heartless Skeletor and, with the help of his Dark Masters, usurped the throne. But Skeletor is not satisfied. The tyrant will not rest until he destroys Castle Grayskull, the mystical lair that channels the cosmic energy at the heart of Eternia.

Until recently, Adam was a sixteen-year-old kid living in the jungles of the Tiger Tribe. He had no memory of the first six years of his life, or his family, until a rebellious young magician named Teela, compelled by strange a voice, brought him a mysterious sword. When Adam raised this Sword of Power and recited certain words, he channeled the energy of Castle Grayskull and transformed into He-Man, the most powerful man in the universe.

Reluctant to keep it to himself, He-Man shared the limitless power of Castle Grayskull with his four good friends, turning Teela into the incomparable Sorceress, Master of Magic; Krass into the unstoppable Ram Ma'am, Master of Demolition; Duncan into Man-at-Arms, Master of Technology; and the aging tiger Cringer into the fearsome Battle Cat, Master of the Wild.

Together, they are the Masters of the Universe, and they are the only ones standing in Skeletor's way.

After a massive battle against the forces of Skeletor resulted in the explosion of the Eternia 2000, the fastest train on the planet[1], Adam, Cringer, Krass, and Duncan have returned to Castle Grayskull. Refusing to abandon his people to Skeletor's reign, King Randor remains in the hidden world of tunnels beneath his city with Teela and the clumsy robo-wizard Ork-0 as his guides and protectors. Meanwhile, in the palace above, Skeletor and his Dark Masters wait impatiently for their next chance to strike.

But the fight on the train has had unintended, unexpected, and extremely unpleasant consequences for the people of Eternia.

THIS IS WHERE OUR STORY BEGINS.

---

1 See Episode 15, "Eternia 2000," of *He-Man and the Masters of the Universe*.

CAST OF CHARACTERS

THE MASTERS OF THE UNIVERSE

HE-MAN: When sixteen-year-old Adam wields the Sword of Power, he transforms into the most powerful man in the universe. On the inside, though, Adam's just a kid feeling the tremendous pressure of his new role. The He-Man thing is only one part of his new life. He recently learned that he's the lost son of King Randor of Eternia, too. Reuniting with his father was weird, but good, yet the whole prince thing doesn't feel right to him. Adam didn't like the idea of keeping the Power of Grayskull to himself, either, so he shared it with his best friends, turning them into the Masters of the Universe.

SORCERESS: The resourceful teenage magician Teela, who first brought the Sword of Power to Adam, channels the Power of Grayskull to become the all-powerful Sorceress. Flight, teleportation, and illusions are only a few of her abilities. Teela and Adam both have mysterious pasts, and Teela will one day learn that her deep connection to Castle Grayskull and its guardian, the sorceress known as Eldress, is far stranger than she could have imagined.

BATTLE CAT: The wise old tiger Cringer found six-year-old Adam abandoned in the jungle, left there by Eldress, the guardian of Grayskull, who was desperate to hide the boy from his evil uncle. For ten years, Cringer raised Adam as one of his own cubs in the Tiger Tribe. Although Adam found his real father eventually, his ties to Cringer are strong, and he wouldn't want to be He-Man without the fearsome Battle Cat at his side. After Duncan forged a new pair of metallic claws for Cringer, who'd lost his natural ones to the brutal poacher Rqazz, Adam infused them with the Power of Grayskull, transforming them into Claws of the Wild.

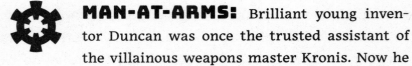

MAN-AT-ARMS: Brilliant young inventor Duncan was once the trusted assistant of the villainous weapons master Kronis. Now he fights at He-Man's side as the tech genius Man-at-Arms, using the Mace of Technology to generate force-field shields, launch drones, and fire missiles. Also known as the Power

Mace, the tool comes in handy when smashing stuff, too, and when Duncan uses his Master Strike, Speed Build, he can slow time to a near standstill and rapidly construct fantastic and complex weapons.

 RAM MA'AM: Brash, exuberant, and arrogant, Krass grew up with Adam in the Tiger Tribe—and those roots mean everything to her. When Adam charges her helmet with Grayskull power, she becomes Ram Ma'am, Master of Demolition. Rocket-enhanced armored boots allow her to race at impossible speeds. Her trusty helmet, which once belonged to her father, morphs into the Helm of Demolition—radiant, crystal-inlaid armor with boosters at the back. And you do *not* want to get in her way.

THE DARK MASTERS

 SKELETOR: Jealous of his brother's reign, the rebellious Prince Keldor set out to steal the Power of Grayskull and take control of Eternos himself. The energy of the castle sensed his evil character and transformed Keldor into Skeletor, the Dark Master of Havoc. Skeletor's staff channels the primordial power of Havoc, enhancing his strength and power, which—along with his devilishly strategic schemes—makes him the one force who could defeat He-Man's effort to protect Eternia.

EVIL-LYN: The Dark Master of Witchcraft was once King Randor's court magician, but she grew frustrated with his refusal to use his full power to rule—and soon swore her allegiance to Keldor, the king's scheming brother. When Skeletor infuses her with Havoc, Evelyn turns into Evil-Lyn, gaining such complete control over the supernatural that she doesn't even need to speak a spell. At this point in the story, however, Evelyn and Skellie have had a little falling out, and the powerful magician is off pursuing a mission of her own.

 TRAP JAW: Once the man-at-arms to King Randor, the weapons master Kronis now serves Skeletor as Trap Jaw, Dark Master of Weaponry. By swallowing existing technology and weapons in his spinning maw, he can quickly create new and more devastating devices. As for that jaw, well, his old assistant Duncan broke it pretty badly when he struck Kronis with his Power Mace during a battle. The devious weapons master is out for revenge, and he wouldn't mind grabbing his old ship back in the process.

BEAST MAN: Former poacher and hunter Rqazz hails from a race of savage bestial-human hybrids called Beastopoids—fierce rivals of Cringer's Tiger Tribe. Now that he's sworn his loyalty to Skeletor, Rqazz has become the fearsome Beast Man, armed with a devastating whip known as the Lash of Beasts, heightened senses, nearly unmatched strength, and the ability to conjure dangerous spirit animals out of thin air. Also, he refers to himself in the third person, and wishes Skeletor would pet him more.

OTHER KEY CHARACTERS

ELDRESS: The spirit of the sorceress who guards Castle Grayskull and helps the heroes understand their new powers and responsibilities. After Skeletor's forces attacked the castle, she channeled the last of her strength to move the fortress to the Sky Kingdom of Avion. Although she saved Grayskull, Eldress herself has disappeared.

KING RANDOR: The latest in a long line of kings to rule over Eternia, Randor was beloved by some, reviled by others. He lost his throne and his kingdom to his scheming brother Keldor, who transformed into the monstrous Skeletor. But Randor has been reunited with his son Adam—the semisecret alter ego of the unstoppable He-Man. For now, Randor's taking a minute, remaining in the hidden world beneath his city to look out for his people, and learn more about them, too.

ORK-0: Part robot, part reincarnated magician, and always accident-prone, Ork-0 is determined to help the Masters of the Universe fight back against Skeletor and the Dark Masters . . . without breaking too much in the process.

MOSS MAN: Eternia's version of Bigfoot, the legendary Moss Man has been roaming the planet for centuries. Members of his species live for thousands of years, but most of them prefer to find a nice home and dig in their roots. Moss Man, whose real name is Kreannot n'Horosh, never stops moving. He has been on the run for four hundred years, but for his kind, he's still only a teenager.

ODIPHUS: Proud, industrious, and entrepreneurial, Odiphus is a Pelleezean, a band of skunk-like humanoids that emit an unfortunate odor. The Pelleezeans are a sad species, forced to roam the planet in search of a home. No matter where they try to settle, the locals force them away because of their stench. Odiphus is determined to change this . . . at any cost.

PRESENT DAY

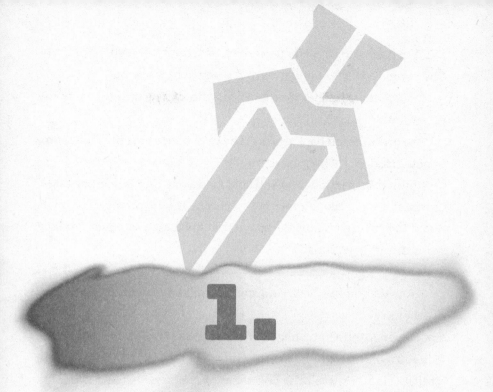

1.

A young girl squinted in the bright morning sunlight. She yawned, sat up in bed, and peered through her window at her beloved flowers in the garden outside.

Dead.

Each and every daisy was dead.

The petals were brown. The stems were withered, sickly stalks that looked as if the life had been sucked right out of them. Yet she'd checked them only the night before! They were perfectly healthy then. Clearly, something terrible had happened in the night.

The girl opened her window. A light morning breeze blew into her room, and although the air was cool, the stench was horrific. Immediately, she staggered back and fell onto the floor. Her nose felt like it was on fire. Her skin seemed to be coated with toxic air. She raced to the foot of her parents' bed across the hall.

The scent struck her mother first, who sprang upright. "Use the bathroom, please!"

The girl pressed back against the wall of her parents' bedroom, beside the door. "That wasn't me!"

Now her father coughed and spat into a cup on his bedside table. "Argh, it smells like a merman's armpit! If I didn't feel like I was about to heave, I'd almost be proud that my daughter could produce something so noxious."

"I didn't do it!"

"How do you know what a merman's armpit smells like?" her mother asked.

"Never mind that," her father snapped. "Don't deny it, child! You're to blame. You never eat your vegetables." His words were muffled as he pressed the bed sheet over his mouth and nose.

"You don't drink enough water, either," her mother added, grabbing the bedsheet away from her husband, "and this is what happens."

The girl stomped one of her bare feet on the wooden floor. "It wasn't me!" she insisted.

Her frustrated parents were about to respond when they noticed something odd about the revolting breeze. There was a thickness to it, a heaviness. And the air was a putrid shade of yellow.

"Really, dear, what *did* you eat?" her mother pressed.

"I told you it wasn't me," the girl exclaimed. "It's coming from outside! It killed my flowers, too."

"Your flowers?" her father replied. "The ones in the garden?" His face turned pale as he turned to his wife. "The corn!"

The family depended on farming, as did everyone else in their village. The three of them rushed outside, each wearing make-shift masks, and stumbled onto a terrible scene. The towering green stalks that had stretched from their house to the woods only the day before were bent over and blackened. Only a small patch of healthy corn remained to the east. The wind shifted. The yellow air swirled toward the last living plants on their land, and the healthy green stalks bent over and died, strangled by the toxic stink.

"Our crop!" the father cried.

"Our farm," the mother muttered.

"My nose," the girl added.

Behind the house, a small hill rose from the landscape. The yellow air swept upward, turning the grass yellow and sending the family's dozen sheep sprinting madly in all directions. The poor creatures ran as if they were being chased by a rabid dog.

The girl dashed up the hill. From the top she could see the other farms that made up their village. At this time of year, the lands were normally a bright, beautiful green. Now, overnight, everything had turned lifeless and brown. The girl gasped. Her father, panting from the run, fell to his knees. A river of toxic air flowed east. Every farm, as far as they could see, was ruined. The girl's father was dumb-founded. If his own crop was dead, he could've hoped to depend on his neighbors. But if everyone in the village had nothing to harvest or sell or trade, what then? How would any of them survive?

"What in the name of King Randor is happening?" the father asked.

"I don't know," the mother responded. "I just don't know."

All across the planet Eternia, similar tragedies were striking families and farms. The noxious yellow wind snaked across the land, twisting and curling east and west, north and south, killing every plant and flower it touched. Tiny flies dropped from the skies. Birds flapped away in panic. Lettuce wilted. Kale crumbled. Potatoes[2] hidden deep in the soil shriveled when the stink brushed against their exposed leaves. Griffins buried their noses in their feathered wings. Sandipedes tunneled deep beneath the desert surface. Even dimwitted navits, which have hardly any sense of smell, hopped into their hiding places out of olfactory disgust.

The girl and her parents remained on top of that hill for some time, staring out at the destruction. Although her father had invoked the name of King Randor, the former ruler of Eternos could not help them now. A new leader sat on his throne in the palace—a brutal, evil, and power-starved villain named Skeletor. The girl and her parents knew little about Skeletor, but based on the news that traveled to their village, they guessed he would not rush to their rescue.

Yet the stories of Skeletor were not the only ones traveling across Eternia in those days. They'd also heard tales of a new team of heroes, a powerful band that was fighting back against Skeletor and his horrifying horde.

Looking off into the distance, the girl raised her head and whispered, "I hope the Masters of the Universe can help us now."

---

2 Eternian potatoes are extremely nutritious and can be eaten raw. Think of them as a cross between carrots and normal, Earth-grown potatoes, but with higher protein content. Adam and Krass both devour them as snacks.

2.

High above the planet Eternia, in the Sky Kingdom of Avion, the legendary Castle Grayskull floated in the clouds. Inside, two boys, a girl, and a very unusual tiger were studying in a vast library. The room, formally known as the Archive of Forbidden Knowledge, wasn't the easiest place to read. The bookshelves floated, and if you leaned your head back in your chair, you'd have a very distracting view of the starry cosmos instead of a standard ceiling.

But the library's current occupants were doing their best to focus. Her head protected inside her beloved helmet, fifteen-year-old Krass was impatiently skimming through a pamphlet on the legends of ancient Eternia. Duncan, a seventeen-year-old genius inventor and former assistant to Skeletor's weapons master, Kronis, was trying to focus on the pages

5

of an old book with yellowed, moldy pages. The wise, aged, and highly intelligent tiger Cringer was poised over a volume of his own, using his metal claws to turn the delicate pages. Adam, sixteen, was yawning and rubbing his eyes as he stood leafing through some similarly intimidating text.

The last few weeks had been interesting ones for Adam. Discovering that he was the lost son of King Randor wasn't even the biggest surprise. Adam had also learned that he'd been chosen to wield a magical weapon called the Sword of Power. When he held this sword and pronounced a few magic words, Adam turned into He-Man, a giant, unstoppable, muscle-bound warrior capable of crushing a boulder with a single punch. The name began as a joke—thanks to Krass—but it was growing on him. As for the power, Adam had no interest in keeping it all to himself. Instead, he shared it with Krass, Duncan, Cringer, and his magician friend Teela, too. By channeling the cosmic energy of Castle Grayskull, each of them transformed into superpowered versions of themselves. Teela became the all-powerful Sorceress. Duncan turned into the Master of Technology, Man-at-Arms. Cringer morphed into the fearsome Battle Cat, and Krass the unstoppable Ram Ma'am.

Together, they were the Masters of the Universe, and at the moment, the four of them in the castle were incredibly bored. There was important work to be done, as the Masters were in the midst of a quest for pieces of a powerful artifact known as the Sigil of Hssss. But the research was wearing on them.

Duncan preferred to be building and tinkering, not confined to a library, and Cringer had known Adam and Krass long enough to see that the pair needed to move. "Why don't you go practice some swordplay, young prince?" Cringer suggested.

Adam shivered. "Please don't call me 'prince.' I'm Adam. Plus, I think I need a little break from the sword."

"How about some fresh air?" Duncan suggested.

"Great idea," Cringer replied. "Careful as you go, though. Grayskull is a castle of many mysteries."

Duncan turned to the library's exit and scratched his chin. "Good point, Cringer. To be honest, I'm not even sure I know how to get back to the jawbridge."

"Don't mean you drawbridge?" Krass asked.

"Nope," Duncan replied. "The front of the castle is a skull, and the bridge is its jaw. Definitely jawbridge."

Krass shrugged. "Race you?"

"Deal!" Duncan said. "But I'm racing Adam and Krass, not He-Man and Rammy."

"And I'm racing Duncan, not Man-at-Arms."

"So building a pair of rocket-powered sky boots would be cheating?"

Krass tapped her helmet. "Unless you want me calling on the Power of Grayskull and firing up my own rockets, yes, that would be cheating."

Before Duncan could respond, Adam leaped up onto the top of the long table in the middle of the library and sprinted for the door.

"Cubs," Cringer warned. "Be careful! This is not a normal castle!"

The archive itself must have been listening. An instant before Krass reached the exit, the huge wooden door slammed shut. She crashed helmet-first and stumbled back to the floor.

Duncan leaned over to check on their friend as Krass sat up, stunned. "No running in the library, I guess," he said. "You're okay?"

Krass nodded. "I'm okay."

"Good," Duncan replied, "because I'm still gonna win."

He walked slowly and carefully to the door, opened it respect-
fully, stepped out into the hall, and sprinted. Adam and Krass
hurried behind him. At the end of the hall, Duncan and Krass
turned left; Adam went right.

The sword at his back was surprisingly small and light. At times
Adam forgot it was there. Halfway down a curving hallway, he stopped
before a painting of King Grayskull himself, the ancient Eternian
ruler who first wielded the Sword of Power. No one had dared use the
sword ever since. Even Adam's father, King Randor, believed it was too
dangerous. Adam chilled at the sight of Grayskull. Did Adam himself
really deserve the sword? Was he even up to the challenge?

Adam gritted his teeth and raced on, but he wasn't really sure
where he was going; he wished Teela was there to show him the way.
Although Adam was the one who was supposed to be connected to
Grayskull and its powers, Teela had a weird feel for the castle and how
it worked. She'd brought the sword to Adam in the first place. Teela
had all the strange Grayskull visions, too. The guardian of the castle,
the sorceress known as Eldress, actually spoke to Teela in her mind.
But Teela couldn't be with them now. She'd stayed back in the capital
city to help his dad. King Randor didn't want to abandon his people,
and Teela didn't think it would be such a great idea to leave the king
alone in the complex maze of tunnels beneath the palace. She knew
the people down there didn't exactly love him, and that he might need
a protector. Still, even though Adam knew she was doing the right
thing, he preferred having her around. Especially inside Grayskull.

The hallway narrowed and bent suddenly to the left.

Okay, Adam decided, I guess I'll go left.

Ahead of him stretched the grand entrance hall, with their ship,
the *Wind Raider*, parked in the center. Adam had passed through

this hall dozens of times already, but it still left him wonderstruck. The tiled floor was scattered with stones and boulders. High walls arched up into space. Much like the archive, the hall had no ceiling. Instead, distant galaxies and stars glowed pink and blue. He stopped, mesmerized—he couldn't help but get distracted. This was supposed to be his home now, but it still didn't feel like one. He figured that was normal, though. Most kids his age didn't have doorways to other dimensions in their front hall.

"I win!" Krass yelled.

Adam shook his head. He'd been so caught up in the mystery of Castle Grayskull that he'd forgotten all about the race, and now his friend stood with her hand on the inside of the stone jawbridge, victorious. Adam laughed. "Next time, no rules."

"You got it, He-Man."

"How about that fresh air?" Adam suggested.

The jawbridge opened gradually.

The three kids closed their eyes and breathed in deep through their noses, savoring the fresh, clean air of Avion. The floating islands of the cloud city stretched out before them, shimmering and glittering in the distance.

Adam felt instantly restored. His energy was renewed. With one breath, everything seemed better and brighter.

The second deep breath was not so delightful.

Duncan coughed. "That's horrible!"

The wind shifted, and Krass leaped away from the doorway, gagging. Adam's eyes teared. His nostrils burned. His stomach soured. The smell blowing into the castle was beyond vile. He wasn't sure if the evil, slovenly Beast Man wore socks, but if he did, they wouldn't smell this rancid. Instinctively, Adam reached

9

for the Sword of Power, then released the handle. What good would a magic sword do him now? He-Man couldn't swat away this horrific stench.

A powerful roar issued from deep inside the castle.

Cringer leaped into the great room, muscles tensed, nose pinched against the odor. "Close the jawbridge now!" he ordered.

Duncan did as he was told, and the four friends watched Castle Grayskull itself fight back against the smell. The yellow air swirled and mixed into a spinning, ball-shaped cloud in the center of the room. A strong breeze rushed out of one of the many hallways, pushing the fetid cloud through the shrinking opening and into the air outside.

Finally, the jawbridge shut, and the four of them breathed.

"What do these Avion people eat?" Duncan asked. "That's the worst gas I've ever smelled in my life, and I hung around with Kronis."

"That was no gas," Cringer growled.

"I recognize that smell," Adam said.

"That odor is Pelleezean," Cringer added.

"The skunk people?" Duncan replied.

"I wouldn't call them that, exactly," Cringer said. "They are a unique species of highly intelligent but admittedly pungent skunk-like humanoids."

"They do stink," Adam added, "but it's kind of sad, because no one wants them around as a result."

"And this is *not* their normal odor," Cringer noted. "Adam, Krass, and I have smelled this particular concoction before, Duncan. It's highly toxic, and if it has spread all the way up here to Avion, the inhabitants of Eternia could be in grave danger."

3.

Castle Grayskull was a mysterious building of many rooms and levels. A door that you walked past in the morning might not be there in the afternoon. The hallways shifted and changed. The kitchen might only be a few steps from the archive one day and a long hike from one level to another the next. There were laboratories, too, but Duncan had forgotten how to find them, and he didn't want to waste any time searching. So, after he gave his friends a list of all the materials he'd need, he suggested they meet in the archive again.

Soon, the four of them were back in the room, breathless. Adam and Cringer dumped a pile of gadgets and electronics on one of the tables. Duncan added a few drones he'd found in the *Wind Raider.* Krass rushed in last, carrying a small chunk of glowing, silver-white quartz.

"That's it?" Duncan asked. "That's all you could find?"

"You should be grateful I found any at all!"

She tossed him the gem. Duncan fumbled the quartz briefly—it bounced from hand to hand. Then he set it down on the table.

"What do you need that for?" Adam asked.

"Well, I'm building two highly sensitive, self-propelling olfactory sensing devices from scratch, and quartz is a good signal conductor."

Krass brushed aside her bangs. "What does that even mean?"

"They're flying artificial noses," Cringer said. "We need them to determine how far this toxic air has spread."

"And we need to do it quickly," Adam noted.

"Can you do your Speed Build thing to hurry it up?" Krass asked. She sprinted across the room, grabbed the inventor's trusted multi-tool wrench, and handed it to him. When Duncan morphed into Man-at-Arms, the tool transformed into an energy-infused Power Mace. The Grayskull magic outfitted him in a pretty sweet armored suit, too. Adam would have been jealous, but given that he himself turned into the most powerful man in the universe, he couldn't really complain.

This time, the young inventor didn't need to call on the Power of Grayskull. Duncan held up one of the artificial noses with two hands, twisted a panel, popped the gem inside, then snapped it shut. "There. Done." Eyeing his latest invention, Duncan began to squint. He cocked his head to one side. "Or at least I think I'm done . . ."

Adam studied his friend. Duncan was one of the smartest, most capable people he'd ever met, but he still lacked confidence in himself. Adam would have to work on that. "I'm sure you did a great job," Adam said, patting his friend on the back.

"One problem, though," Duncan added.

"What's that?" Krass asked.

"We'll need at least a hundred if we want to cover all of Eternia and I don't have enough quartz."

"There is a sizable vein of quartz buried beneath Snake Mountain," Cringer started.

"Um, no thanks," Duncan interrupted. "I'm not exactly eager to get back to Skeletor's old clubhouse anytime soon."

Adam pointed to Cringer. "How do you even know that?" he asked.

"We're in a library, Adam," the tiger replied. "You'd be surprised what you can learn when you read. I did a little research on Snake Mountain before our last adventure."

Hands on his hips, staring up at the stars overhead, Duncan announced that they could figure out the quartz shortage later. "First we need to see if these prototypes actually work."

"Of course they'll work!" Adam said, slapping his friend on the back again. "You're a genius."

The inventor winced, not quite sharing Adam's faith in his abilities, and Cringer reminded them that launching one of the devices from inside the archive wouldn't do any good. They wanted the prototypes to soar over the planet Eternia, not fly off to some distant galaxy or another dimension. So the four Masters hurried up to the top of one of the lookout towers.

The first time Adam had been up here, he'd been searching for Grayskull's bathroom, and the tower had offered a view of a desolate landscape. Now, though, they were surrounded by the floating islands, glimmering palaces, and shimmering cloudfalls of the Sky Kingdom of Avion. Adam paused in amazement. All of this was still so new to him.

He could have stood there and stared for hours.

But they weren't there to marvel at the view.

Duncan launched the flying sensor, and the Masters immediately ran back to the archive. Next, Duncan activated a digital, three-dimensional representation of Eternia. The holo-globe appeared in mid-air above the main table. Adam marveled at all the territories—the Harmony Seas, the now-deserted Trollan Plains, Selkie Island, the Mystic Mountains, all the sprawling forests and vast, unforgiving deserts. Suddenly, the tremendous pressure of his new role as champion struck him as powerfully as Skeletor's bony left fist.

As He-Man, he was supposed to protect this planet.

The whole thing.

Adam gulped.

Duncan updated the program that generated the display, connecting it to the flying artificial nose. Soon, yellow rivers of air snaked across the farmlands below them. Krass mumbled a question. Adam, too. But Duncan and Cringer ignored them both, watching as more yellow clouds and lines appeared. The toxic air was spreading fast.

"That is *not* good," Krass said, staring at the digital globe.

"It's worse than I feared," Cringer added. "If that poisoned wind continues to spread, it could devastate farms across the planet. Millions of Eternians could starve. We must do something. Adam, can you use the sword to contact Teela?"

He wasn't sure. The last time Adam had to make that kind of emergency call, he'd talked to Eldress through the sword, convincing her to summon the last of her powers to move Castle Grayskull and save it from destruction. Would the trick work with Teela, too? She did have that uncanny link to the castle.

"I guess I could try," he said at last. "Why?"

"Because we need all the help—and all the information—we can get," Cringer replied.

Adam stood, backed away from his seat, and held the sword before him.

Closing his eyes and concentrating, he said, "Teela, can you hear me?"

The handle of the weapon vibrated slightly.

His hands and forearms tingled.

Then he heard a familiar voice in his head. "Is that you, Adam?"

"Whoa, it worked?! Yes, Teela, it's me."

A radiant blue light shone near the door, and Teela appeared as a ghost-like projection. Adam was beyond impressed with how much she'd grown into her powers already. Sure, when he'd first met Teela, she could already sneak through the capital city unnoticed, fight soldiers, and pull off all kinds of magic tricks. But ever since she'd inherited the staff that had belonged to Eldress, Teela had discovered a whole new set of powers. The silver-gray staff was pretty sweet looking, too.

"What's up?" Teela asked. "I'm kind of busy. I don't have much time."

"What have you heard about the toxic air?"

"I thought you might be wondering about that," Teela answered. "Down here in the tunnels we don't normally worry much about what's happening on the farms. The people here have their own problems. But that stench is leaking down into the Lower Wards, too."

"Is it Skeletor?" Cringer asked.

"No, I don't think Skeletor's behind it. From what I'm hearing, he has two things on his mind right now: destroying Castle Grayskull and throwing himself a birthday party."

"So is it some kind of natural disaster?" Krass wondered.

"Or an accident?" Adam asked.

"Might be a little of both, actually," Teela replied. "The story I'm hearing down here is that it has to do with your dad, Adam. Apparently, a Pelleezean came to him a little while back with what he insisted was a gift of the most beautiful perfume ever made. Your dad didn't want to insult him, so he accepted, but when one of his pages tested the scent, the poor guy fainted immediately, and was confined to a hospital bed for a week. So King Randor stashed the remains of the perfume in the royal vault."

"Don't tell me it ended up on the *Eternia 2000*," Krass said.

"I'm guessing that's exactly what happened," Teela replied.

The four friends inside Grayskull quietly digested the news. The *Eternia 2000* had been the planet's fastest and most advanced train. Before Skeletor invaded his palace, King Randor had ordered his guards to empty the royal vault and transfer all of the contents to the train. While this had seemed like a good plan at the time, since the villainous tyrant desperately wanted the powerful relics and weapons stashed inside, Randor hadn't anticipated that the *Eternia 2000* would be the site of a great battle between the forces of He-Man, Skeletor, and the notorious bandit Mosquit'ra. In the chaos of the fight, the contents of the royal vault had been thrown all across the planet as the compartments of the speeding train exploded one at a time.

All the contents—including that toxic perfume.

Adam could barely breathe.

And not because of any lingering remains of the odor.

He was sick with guilt. His father wasn't the only one who'd encountered this particular Pelleezean parfumier. Adam had met the creature himself years earlier. Not only that—he'd actually encouraged the Pelleezean to develop that perfume. If Teela's information was accurate, this whole mess was his fault.

"Did you ask my dad?" Adam pressed. "What did he say?"

The ghostly projection of their friend flickered, and Teela completely ignored his question. "Sorry," she said, "I really do have to go."

"Wait!" Duncan said, moving in front of the projection. He held up one of his gloved fingers. "I have a favor to ask." The inventor held up the second prototype. "I need about a hundred more of these, but I don't have the raw materials to build enough of them. Any chance you could, you know . . ."

"Do that witchy thing you do?" Krass asked, finishing for him.

With a skeptical growl, Cringer shook his huge head. "I fear that might be too powerful a spell for our friend to cast from such a great distance, Duncan."

"You might be right, Cringer," Teela noted, "but I'll give it a try."

Adam watched with awe as an odd look came over Teela. She bowed her head slightly. With two hands, she raised the Grayskull-powered staff. The blue diamond in the center glowed. A bluish-purple light radiated all around her. When Teela transformed into Sorceress, her staff changed, too, and you could see the distant stars and galaxies in its winged, falcon-shaped head. This time, his friend didn't power up, so Adam couldn't see the cosmos in the staff, but it obviously still had tremendous strength. Everything around Teela shone brighter.

She jammed the staff down against the floor.

The glow faded instantly.

She opened her eyes wide. "Well? Did it work?"

Before Adam could answer, the prototype in Duncan's hands suddenly doubled, sprouting a twin. Then those two doubled. The process repeated over and over, second by second, until there were so many satellites that they spilled off the table, bouncing onto the floor.

Yes, Adam decided, the spell had definitely worked.

And Teela was growing even more powerful than he'd realized.

"Amazing," Cringer murmured. "Absolutely amazing."

"Not bad, witchy," Krass added. "Not bad at all!"

Teela blinked and surveyed the results of her spell. "Sorry," she said, "that might be more than a hundred."

Duncan picked up one of the cloned gadgets. "No problem," he muttered, his voice slightly higher pitched. Adam smiled—his friend was so stunned he couldn't think of quite how to respond. Duncan turned the magically replicated sensor around in his hands and popped open a panel to peer inside. "Ha! Quartz! Never thought I'd be so excited to see quartz. Thank you, Teela!"

"You're welcome," Teela said. "But now I *really* have to go. Good luck!"

"Teela, wait!" Adam called to her, but his friend had already vanished.

Why was she in such a rush? He'd wanted to ask her about his father. She and the clumsy robo-wizard Ork-0 were supposed to be protecting the king, but Adam hadn't seen either of them with her. And she'd pretended like she hadn't even heard his question about his dad. But he told himself not to worry. King Randor would be fine. He was the rightful ruler of Eternos. Surely he could survive a few days in the tunnels beneath the city.

Adam had bigger things to think about.

If Cringer was right, millions of lives depended on him and his friends.

He breathed in slowly, silently wondering if he was up to the challenge.

4.

Duncan leaned over with both hands lying flat on the table. He scanned the pile of satellites and frowned. Then he stood back and scratched his head. "Okay, so if we want to see where the toxic gas is spreading, we need these to be flying all over Eternia. I guess we could take the *Wind Raider* and cruise around the planet, dropping them off as we go—"

Krass interrupted. "No. That would take too long."

Stumped, Duncan grabbed one of the satellites and tossed it up to himself a few times. On the fourth throw, Adam snagged the artificial nose out of the air. With a confident smirk, he said, "I've got an idea."

Adam placed the sensor down on the table, reached over his shoulder, and removed the Sword of Power. He gripped the golden hilt with both of his small, skinny hands, breathed deeply, and held the mystical weapon over his head. Then he pronounced the words that had changed everything for him.

"BY THE POWER OF GRAYSKULL . . ."

Instantly, the world around him disappeared. The archive and its floating bookshelves and cosmic ceiling were gone. All that remained was his sixteen-year-old self and pure energy. Lightning exploded all around him. The power of Castle Grayskull flowed through the sword and into his hands, coursing through his arms, into his chest and back, down through his legs. The energy looked like some kind of golden fire, but it didn't burn in the slightest. Instead, it enlivened him. He felt as if every cell in his body had been injected with fantastic cosmic power. His skin stretched. His bones widened and strengthened. Every muscle expanded. A strange warmth spread through him, and he grew from a scrawny teenager into a muscular giant in seconds. Thankfully, he still had great hair, too.

When the transformation was complete, and the incomparable strength of Grayskull pulsed in his every fiber, Adam extended his sword and added, "I HAVE THE POWER!"

The golden energy dispersed.

The interior of the castle, and his friends staring at him, returned to view.

Krass shook her helmeted head. "Still weird," she said. "I've seen that a few times now, but it's still weird."

"Yep," Duncan agreed. "Super cool, too."

"Why are you powering up, He-Man?" Cringer asked, using Adam's other name—the name of Eternia's great champion. "I don't see Skeletor around."

He-Man grabbed an armful of the devices and raced back up to the top of the tower. His friends followed. With the skies above Eternos stretching out before him, he hurled one of the devices as hard as he could. His three friends watched, momentarily confused, before Duncan understood his plan. The young inventor tapped at a handheld computer and switched on a smaller holographic projection of the planet. The yellow clouds of gas from the first artificial nose showed in the same section, but within a few seconds, another cloud appeared hundreds of miles away. "Whoa!" Duncan exclaimed. "That worked! How fast did you throw that thing? Light speed?"

He-Man shrugged his huge shoulders. "No idea. Toss me another one."

Quickly, the group divided up their tasks. Krass ran back and forth to the archive, grabbing as many of the satellites as she could, and Cringer rolled them to He-Man one at a time. Consulting his digital holo-globe, Duncan looked for the areas that hadn't yet been covered by an artificial nose, calculated the direction and distance, and informed He-Man where to throw and with how much strength. This last part took a little adjusting—at one point, He-Man accidentally hurled one of the satellites out of Eternia's orbit and into the darkness of space. Duncan joked that they'd now be able to answer the age-old question of whether the stars smell.

He-Man laughed. Nearly every other time Adam had transformed into the giant warrior, he'd done so because of an emergency or a fight. Now he was testing his abilities without that same pressure.

He was actually having fun.

He'd hurled at least a hundred of the gadgets when Duncan finally told him to stop. "That's perfect," the inventor proclaimed, hurrying down the stairs.

Back inside the archive, Duncan shut down the hologram, then rebooted the system as He-Man powered down in a flash into his scrawnier, normal self. "Thanks to the big dude, our artificial noses are all over Eternia. Once the hologram comes back online, it should show us all the places on the planet that have been impacted by the toxic air."

The program worked as Duncan hoped, but the results were chilling.

The toxic wind had already spread across half of Eternia.

Cringer growled. "This could prove devastating."

"What do we do?" Adam asked.

Duncan started to pace. "We need to find a way to stop it."

"We can't forget about the Sigil of Hssss," Krass reminded them.[3]

"Agreed," Cringer responded, "but our quest for those sigil pieces is temporarily at an impasse. For now, this toxic air is a more pressing problem."

Adam started to reach for the sword again, but the weapon wouldn't be much help. He couldn't just smack a current of air with his blade. Adam pointed at Duncan. "What if you build something?"

"Right! Something that could reverse the damage," Krass added.

---

3 Protecting the planet is a busy job. The Masters are also searching for the scattered pieces of the Sigil of Hssss, a magical weapon with the power to raise an army of undead soldiers, and they need to find them before Skeletor and his minions. See Episode 11 of *He-Man and the Masters of the Universe* for more!

"Sure, okay . . ." Duncan replied. "Let me just see if I can find the old Planet Saver 5000 and then—"

"Sarcasm won't save anyone," Cringer said.

"Sorry," Duncan replied. "You're right. It's just, well . . . I need to know more about this toxic breeze before I can come up with a way to stop it or reverse the changes."

Cringer looked at Adam and Krass. "There is someone who might be able to help us," the tiger suggested. "Most Eternians call him Moss Man."

The four of them were silent for a moment. Then Duncan started laughing. "Moss Man? Are you serious? You're talking about the fifty-foot-tall tree guy, right? He's a legend!"

"No," Krass replied. "He's not."

"He's very real indeed," Cringer added. "His real name is Kreannot n'Horosh and he is not fifty feet tall. He's closer to the size of a large man. His species, Floranians, are fascinating creatures. They live for thousands and thousands of years. Kreannot himself should be about four hundred years old by now, but for a Floranian, he's still only a teenager."

"Huh," Duncan responded, "I've never met a four-hundred-year-old kid before." He paused. "You're serious, aren't you?" The giant tiger growled. "Okay," Duncan continued. "Got it. There's a Moss Man. So how do we find him? I'm guessing you know where he lives, right?"

Adam stared at the holo-globe and the many lands stretching across Eternia. "It's not that simple. He could be anywhere."

"Wait, you know about him, too, Adam?" Duncan breathed out heavily. He held up his hands, then wrang them together. "Okay.

Let's back up for a minute. Why do you think this plant dude can help us? What else do you know about him? And *how* do you even know anything about him at all?"

"We met him once," Krass said with a shrug.

"A few times, in my case," Cringer noted.

"We learned some interesting things about him," Adam added.

"*And* about each other," Krass noted.

Duncan settled back into a chair, swung his feet up onto the table, and joined his hands behind his head. "Okay. Let's hear it. If we're going to solve this problem, you need to tell me everything."

"Everything?" Krass asked.

"Everything."

Adam glanced over at Cringer. "We have to go back two years, to when we were still in the tribe."

"Go ahead," Duncan replied. "I'm listening."

"Well," Adam began, "I guess it all started the night before we were due to get our stripes . . ."

TWO YEARS EARLIER

THE JUNGLE HOME OF
THE TIGER TRIBE

5.

The village of the Tiger Tribe was in a frenzy. Every adult cat and human was busily preparing for the next day's festivities. Long tables were set with silver bowls for the tigers, plus plates and goblets for the humanoid members of the tribe. Drums were arranged on the bandstand. A small stage for the honored guests had been rolled out into the middle of the central village square. Tigers and people were arguing over how to string the lanterns across the clearing as fourteen-year-old Adam peered out through his window, watching it all.

This was the start of his eighth year in the tribe. Cringer, one of the older tigers, had found him abandoned in the jungle when he was just six years old. Back then, Adam had no memory of his early life. He didn't know where he'd come from or whether he even had parents and a family of his own. The only clue to his royal roots was the oversize, golden, bracelet-like cuff on his wrist, but no member of the tribe actually suspected he was a prince.

Once a year, the tribe hosted a ceremony to induct new members into their family. The party was filled with music and food and games; it lasted almost an entire day. The ceremony was always one of the highlights of the year, especially for Adam's friend Krass.

This one was different, though. Krass and Adam wouldn't just be watching. They were the two guests of honor. The ceremony, the feast, the music—it was all for them. The Tiger Tribe had been treating Adam like one of their own since that day Cringer found him, and now they were going to make it official. The next night, he was going to get his stripes. How could he be expected to sleep?

Adam was the ideal age for a human to be inducted into the tribe. Krass was a little young, but she was so eager to join that the elders made an exception. Unlike Adam, she still remembered her family, and the terrible crash that ended their lives, leaving her alone and stranded in the jungle. The Tiger Tribe rescued her and raised her like one of their own cubs. Now Krass was eager to return the sentiment, swear her allegiance, and earn her stripes.

So, naturally, she couldn't sleep, either.

Adam heard the thin door between their small rooms brush against the dirt floor of their hut. "I can hear you," he said.

"I can't sleep," she confessed, hurrying over to sit at the foot of his cot.

"Me, neither," Adam admitted.

The main door to the hut swung open as Cringer softly padded inside. "Don't be nervous, cubs," he said. "You're both ready for the honor, and there are signs that tomorrow will be momentous. The sky is filled with stars. The jungle is quiet. There's even a chance that we might have a special guest at the ceremony tomorrow. One of our sentries spotted signs of Moss Man in the woods."

Adam and Krass both laughed at first, thinking the tiger was joking, or telling them some kind of fantastical bedtime story. Yet Cringer insisted that Moss Man was real.

"No way!" Krass shouted. "I heard he can crush a building by wrapping it in one of his branches!"

Cringer laughed quietly. "I'm not sure if that's true," he replied. "I never saw him do that, anyway."

"Wait," Adam said, sitting up, "you know him?"

"Yes. Years ago, when I was a cub, I knew Moss Man well. His real name is Kreannot n'Horosh."

"Seriously? How are we supposed to remember that?"

Adam tried to think of a suggestion. "It rhymes with . . . nothing."

"He's Moss Man," Krass decided. "Let's stick to that."

The tiger nodded and settled into a more comfortable position on the ground, one foreleg resting atop the other. Krass and Adam joined him on the floor of the hut, leaning back against Adam's cot as they listened. "You were really friends with him?" Adam asked.

Cringer nodded and began his story. "One day, long ago, he raced into our village. He'd left the patch of forest where he first sprouted roots in hopes of seeing more of our beautiful planet. When we met, he'd just come from the Badlands—a terrifying, lonely, desolate place that I hope neither of you ever has to see. I suppose our village and tribe were attractive to him after spending time in such a barren wasteland. We taught him our ways and played simple games. One morning, we played hide-and-seek. My friends and I found each other, one by one, but by the end of that day we still hadn't discovered Kreannot. A few of the tribal elders insisted that Moss Man must have continued on his journey, so we gave up searching."

"And that was it?"

"No, Krass. You didn't let me finish."

"So then what happened?"

"A month later, the same friends and I were playing in a beautiful tree outside the village. We knew the jungle well, but we'd never noticed this tree before, and we were climbing and leaping around its trunk when it suddenly shook us free. In a low, rumbling voice, it asked, 'Did I win?'"

"Moss Man didn't move?" Adam asked.

"Seriously?" Krass replied. "He played for a month?"

"Time is different for his kind," Cringer continued. "Members of his species live for thousands of years. A month for Kreannot was like an hour for us. We cheered our new friend and soon the whole tribe had come out to celebrate his victory. He was swinging cubs from his branches and tossing them playfully into the air. He really did feel like family. The elders of the tribe were so enamored with our new friend that they offered him a place among us."

Krass jumped to her feet and clapped her hands together. "Moss Man is Tiger Tribe? That's epic!"

"Let me finish, Krass. He was *almost* Tiger Tribe. The ceremony was already due to take place the next day. The village square was decorated as it is now. The entire tribe was ready to give him his stripes. The night before, I went to check on him, and found that he was in the midst of uprooting himself. The transformation was startling. The branches the cubs had been swinging on retracted. His roots combined and formed humanlike legs, and he slowly assumed his former shape—half boy, half plant. When he saw me, he tried to run. But I was one of the fastest cubs in the tribe. I raced past him and blocked his way. I asked where he was going, and he admitted that he was planning to flee. Naturally, I was hurt. As you both know, earning one's stripes is a great honor, and he was rejecting that chance."

"How ungrateful!" Krass said.

"Maybe it didn't feel right to him," Adam countered. "Maybe he felt like it wasn't really his home."

Cringer eyed him curiously before continuing. "I asked him, but Kreannot never explained why he left. Still, he returns now and then, passing through the jungle quickly, never settling long enough for his roots to take hold. I wouldn't be surprised if the rumors are true and he really is in the jungle tonight. Someday I'll show you the place where he established his roots. It's near the winding stream off the northern path. There's a small mound sprouting all kinds of different flowers and herbs. It's a sacred place for me, and a reminder of the sanctity of home and family."

They lay in silence for a while until Cringer stomped a paw against the ground. "Now, enough tales of Moss Man. The two of you need sleep. You have a big day ahead of you tomorrow!"

The tiger left their hut.

The village soon turned quiet.

Well, mostly quiet. Krass was snoring like a pond-dwelling phribian[4]. And Adam couldn't sleep. He rolled onto one side, then the other. The golden cuff slid down his wrist. As part of the

---

4 A noisy frog-like creature common to Eternian ponds and estuaries.

ceremony, he was expected to sacrifice something from his former life, and the mysterious golden cuff was the obvious choice. But Adam wasn't ready to give it away. He loved the Tiger Tribe. Cringer had become like a father to him. Or a very furry uncle, anyway. And Krass was like a little sister. An often annoying but ultimately endearing sibling. Yet some part of him hoped that he would find his family again one day.

His real family.

And his real home, too.

Was that why Moss Man had fled?

Was he looking for his home?

Adam rolled back from one side of his bed to the other, certain this was going to be a sleepless night. His window was open. The cool night air flowed into the hut, and he decided there was only way to find out why the legendary creature had chosen not to join the tribe.

Adam had to find Moss Man himself.

He crept out of the hut quietly, then followed the northern path out of the village. There was no guarantee Moss Man would return to the spot where he'd once rooted himself. Adam wasn't even certain the creature was in the jungle at all. But the place Cringer had described would be a good starting point, at least.

Adam ran at a steady pace.

Swinging from vine to vine was faster, but he hadn't mastered that yet.

The jungle grew darker by the minute. Tall trees blocked the night sky. Near the Tiger Tribe's base, the jungle floor was wide open and clear, but here dense growth packed both sides of the trail. Adam was about to stop for a breath when he heard the sound of slowly flowing water. He broke off the path and into the brush. Pushing his way through, he followed the noise to the winding stream, then hurried along its edge. He could feel his pulse pounding.

At a bend in the stream, he came to a clearing with a high dirt mound in the center. He stepped closer. The mound was covered with thick green moss. He pressed his hand into the moss, then lifted it away and watched as the imprint of his fingers slowly disappeared.

The clearing was quiet, peaceful—and it smelled terrible!

Adam gagged as a horrible odor filled the air.

Did Moss Man have a gas problem?

Adam stumbled away from the mossy mound, but the stench was all around him. He backtracked blindly. One of his heels caught on something.

He lost his balance.

Suddenly, the ground beneath him fell away.

Adam plummeted backward into darkness.

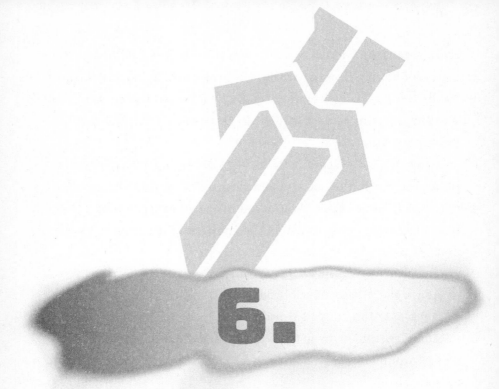

6.

He crashed to the bottom of an earthen pit, slamming his shoulder into the dirt. When he sat up, he was tangled in a mess of branches, leaves, and netting. A wet leaf was plastered to the side of his face. He peeled it off, pulled a few sticks out of his hair, stood up, and studied his surroundings. The pit was twice as deep as he was tall. The rim was far out of reach, and the sides were all mud and dirt with no handholds. Even the roots sticking out of the soil had been severed. There was no hope of climbing out.

Above him, an unfamiliar voice called out, "Got you!"

The foul stench strengthened as an orange light glowed above him. A torch extended out over the rim of the pit, held there by an arm covered in thick black hair. Not a human arm, either. Slowly, the creature came into view, and Adam had never seen anything like it.

The beast had two arms and two legs and stood about as tall as a normal human adult. Its eyes were small but bright, and its slightly open mouth revealed a set of razor-sharp teeth. The nose of the animal was brownish black, rough-skinned, and it stood out prominently on the creature's face. But what truly distinguished the creature was the thick coat of black hair that covered its entire body, including most of its face, and the wide white stripe that extended from the top of its head, down its back, and up along its thick, long tail.

Adam nearly jumped. "Skunk!"

The creature snarled. "I am *not* a skunk. And you are not Moss Man! What are you doing in my trap? This isn't for humans!"

Adam was startled; the animal sounded like a person. "Sorry," he said. "I didn't mean to fall in here. But wait . . . you're trying to catch Moss Man?"

"Yes! And you're ruining everything! Plus, why are you looking at me so strangely? Haven't you ever seen one of my kind before?"

"Ummm, no. What are you, exactly?"

"I am Odiphus," the creature said, turning to reveal the full length of his thick tail, "and this glorious appendage should help you recognize my species."

Adam shrugged. "Sorry. No clue."

"I'm a Pelleezean! What do they teach you in school?"

"I'm in school with a bunch of tigers," Adam explained. "Mostly we learn about leadership, teamwork, hunting, and grooming. Last year I learned how to lick my hands clean. It's weird but effective."

The Pelleezean paused for a moment. "Well, since you are so uneducated, I will do you the honor of introducing my race. We are a highly intelligent species. We're skilled diggers and trappers, as you see," he added, motioning proudly at the pit, "but humans find us revolting due to our unique odor. Whenever we try to settle in a new home, you sensitive humans chase us away. We're not naturally nomadic, but you *humans* force us to wander Eternia."

Adam crinkled his nose. The smell was definitely terrible, but he didn't want to offend Odiphus. He felt bad for the Pelleezeans, too. That would be horrible to have people chasing you out of every-place you tried to settle. "I don't know what bothers them," Adam said. "I don't notice anything."

The Pelleezean planted his torch into the dirt beside him. The flame glowed over the pit. His yellow eyes narrowed. "Really? You don't find my scent repulsive?"

Adam didn't want to lie. But he didn't want to hurt the Pelleez-ean's feelings, either, even if the creature did currently have him trapped in an inescapable pit. Adam shrugged. "It's certainly not worth chasing you out of your home for," he said. "I could get used to it."

For a moment, Odiphus studied him quietly. Then, mutter-ing, the Pelleezean reached into a bag slung over his shoulder. He removed a small glass bottle with a nozzle on top. "It's funny you should say that about getting used to the smell," he began. "I figured maybe the problem is that humans don't smell *enough* of us, you know? They're turned off because they're not accustomed to our naturally magnificent odor. So I created a more concentrated version of our scent." He tossed the bottle down to Adam, who caught it. "What do you think?"

Adam turned the glass vial around in his hands. There was no label. No name, either. "Cool bottle," he said. "How's it selling?"

"Terribly," Odiphus confessed. "I'm guessing it's a marketing problem. At first I wanted to call it Scent of the Woods, maybe, or the Odor of Odiphus. Neither worked very well, though. My latest idea is a little different. What do you think of Stinkor?"

Adam couldn't think of how to respond to that. Would it be possible to think of a worse name? No, probably not. But he didn't want to hurt the Pelleezean's feelings. So he nodded along silently.

Odiphus stood at the edge of the pit and gazed up into the air as if he were picturing the banner of an illuminated advertising head-line shining above the city of Eternos. "I can almost see the tagline," Odiphus continued. "*Stinkor: Nature's Most Pungent Perfume.*" He swung back around and faced Adam. "One day, everyone in Eternos will be spraying themselves." Suddenly comfortable, Odiphus sat on the rim of the dirt prison. His huge feet dangled over the side. They were padded at the bottom, not hairy, and thick, pointy claws extended out from each of his toes instead of nails. "I'm still work-ing on the formula, though," Odiphus said. "The current version has some unfortunate side effects."

"Like what?" Adam asked.

"It kind of kills plant life."

"Kind of?"

"No," Odiphus admitted. "Definitely. I'll work out the kinks even-tually. I'll find a way for us to settle somewhere." Then he sighed and shook his head. "I'll tell you, it's not easy being Pelleezean."

Adam ran one of his fingers along the dirt wall of the pit. "I can only imagine. It's not all that great being trapped in here, either. Would you mind letting me out?"

Odiphus lifted a paw to his forehead, then dropped a rope down into the pit. "I'm so sorry! I should've thrown that down earlier. And hurry, too, if you don't mind. I need to rebuild the trap to catch my prey."

Adam pocketed the perfume, grabbed the rope, yanked on it twice to test that it was secure, and planted his feet on the side of the pit. Leaning back, he walked his way up as he gripped the rope, hand over hand. When he finally reached the top, Odiphus quickly set to work resetting the trap. "Why *are* you trying to catch Moss Man?" Adam asked. "And how do you know he's here?"

As Odiphus pulled the net tight over the pit, then scattered leaves and brush across the top, he began to explain. "Because I tracked him here. I've been tracking him for years! You see, I need him. My fellow Pelleezeans need him. Or, more precisely, we need his mossflowers."

"What's a mossflower?" Adam asked.

"They bloom on his body."

"Like chest hair?"

"What's chest hair?"

"Never mind."

Odiphus looked at him curiously before continuing. "His mossflowers counteract our natural Pelleezean scent. I've seen their power at work once before. A large group of us Pelleezeans had settled on the outskirts of the Mystic Mountains. We thought our human neighbors would chase us away as usual, but Moss Man was in the area at the time. His mossflowers were blooming, too, and the humans didn't complain once! We were all quite happy."

"What happened?" Adam asked.

Odiphus stopped his work and shrugged. "He left. And when he left, the humans turned on us immediately."

"That's terrible," Adam replied, as much to himself as to the Pelleezean. Getting chased from place to place was no way to live.

"Yes, but I'm going to fix it tonight," Odiphus declared. "I'm going to see to it that Moss Man sets his roots near my fellow Pelleezeans, and for the first time in centuries, we'll be able to remain in one place, without humans chasing us away. We'll actually have a real home."

The goal was noble; Adam wouldn't argue that. Everyone deserved a home. But there was one big problem with the plan. "What if he doesn't want to go with you?"

Odiphus held up both paws. "Toss me back that perfume, if you don't mind?" Adam reached into his pocket and handed the Pelleezean the bottle. Odiphus motioned for him to step back, then sprayed a single, careful puff into the air. Instantly, the ferns, weeds, and other plants in the clearing withered and browned.

Adam's eyes teared. He forced back a gag and gritted his teeth.

"I'll give him a choice," Odiphus explained. "He can come with me and do as I say, or I'll unleash my potent perfume on this jungle and kill every plant within miles."

A frightening chill had taken over the Pelleezean's tone. Adam was certain he'd deliver on the threat, and he couldn't let Odiphus do that. The jungle was the home of the Tiger Tribe, and Adam had to protect it. He had to talk the Pelleezean out of his plan, and he guessed that appealing to the proud creature's vanity was his best option. "I don't know," Adam said. "That *might* work, but I like your perfume idea better. If everyone gets used to your smell, then you can live wherever you want. All you need is a few famous people to use it. Maybe a Moduluk[5] player? Or the king! If the king uses your perfume, everyone will follow. Pretty soon all of Eternia will smell like a Pelleezean, and no one will be chasing you away." Adam watched as Odiphus circled the mound, thinking. "I say forget Moss Man," Adam said. "Go with your perfume plan instead."

The Pelleezean considered Adam's suggestion in silence. Adam even thought he'd convinced the scheming skunk-man. Then a devilish glint appeared in the creature's yellow eyes. "Or I could have the best of both worlds," Odiphus mused. "I could capture Moss Man *and* become a titan of the perfume industry. I could be the most powerful Pelleezean on the planet and—"

A vine as thick as a man's leg swung down out of the treetops and slammed against the Pelleezean's back, knocking him to the ground. A second, thinner vine wrapped itself around the handle of the torch, grabbing it from Odiphus, then shoving it straight down into the middle of the nearby stream. The water hissed and steamed as the flame was extinguished. Then Adam watched as a small pink flower with weak blue lines around its petals floated down from the treetops. Two more vines extended out of the darkness, grabbing and then pulverizing the flower, and a light breeze spread the dust around the clearing.

---

5 An extremely popular Eternian sport in which a round ball is carried between players' feet and contestants are only allowed to walk or run on their hands. Wrist and back injuries are common; the players' careers are short but illustrious.

Instantly, the once dead greenery all around them sprang back to life.

Furious, Odiphus leaped to his feet, clawing at the mysterious branch. "Let me go! Give me one of those mossflowers!"

More vines snaked out of the brush, wrapping around the Pelleezean's hairy arms and legs. Odiphus was pinned to the jungle floor as an old, powerful voice rumbled out from the darkness. "Leave this place tonight and never return," the voice said, "or I'll see to it that you lie here for a hundred years."

"Give me one of your flowers, Moss Man!" Odiphus snarled.

"Leave this jungle now!" the voice roared.

The vines around the Pelleezean's legs tightened. Odiphus winced in pain. "Fine! I'll go! Let me free!" His living chains loosened. The panicking Pelleezean leaped to his feet and bared his teeth at the shadows. As he ran off into the darkness, he shouted, "You've not smelled the last of me, Moss Man!"

Adam watched the scene in awe. His hands were shaking. He scanned the jungle floor around him, hoping none of the strange vines were growing toward him. Backing out of the clearing, Adam tried to explain himself. "I wasn't trying to trap you, Kreannot," he insisted, "but I was trying to find you. I have a question."

A brief silence followed.

Then Kreannot replied, "You know my name."

His voice had changed, turning younger. "You sound like a kid," Adam noted.

"Because I am one," Kreannot said. He laughed, and it sounded like hundreds of twigs snapping. "That wasn't my normal voice.

I was trying to come across as older. More legendary, you know? Did it work?"

"Totally," Adam said. He still couldn't actually see Kreannot. The creature probably didn't want to be seen, he guessed. "So, I'm Adam and I'm Tiger Tribe," he explained. "Or almost, anyway. That's what I wanted to talk to you about." He swallowed. He had the creature's attention; now was the time to ask. "I heard you were going to get your stripes, but you decided against it. Why?"

"The tribe was good to me," Kreannot said after a pause, "but receiving my stripes would have meant this jungle was my true home. I couldn't accept that."

"Why not?"

"Because it's not my home!" Kreannot admitted. "I'm happiest when I'm moving, exploring some new land on this beautiful world. I see *all* of Eternia as my home."

Adam paused. What an odd thing to say! How could an entire planet be your home? He didn't understand what that meant.

Yet the idea appealed to him, somehow, on a stranger, deeper level.

"If the whole planet's your home, why are you back here?"

"I still feel a connection to this jungle and the tribe," Kreannot added. "I like visiting, but that doesn't mean it's my home."

Adam looked off into the woods. He thought of the fleeing Pelleezean and his own search for a home for his kind. Adam definitely didn't approve of the way Odiphus wanted to fix things for the Pelleezeans, but they deserved a place to live as much as anyone else. And Kreannot had the power to help him. "Why couldn't you just give one of your mossflowers to Odiphus?"

42

"He was threatening this jungle," Kreannot answered. "I don't take kindly to threats."

"Can't you just make him another one?"

"No, it doesn't work like that," Kreannot replied. "That was my last one, and my flowers only bloom when I'm happy. I don't trust that Pelleezean, either. These trees and plants are my friends. My family. I need to protect them, so I need to see to it that he does leave this jungle immediately. Goodbye, Adam, and good luck!"

7.

An instant after Kreannot disappeared into the darkness, an enormous tiger leaped out of the brush. Cringer growled, then stepped forward with Krass at his side. Next, he sat back on his haunches, turning his huge head from side to side. "Who's there?" the tiger roared. "Adam, are you hurt?"

"I'm fine," Adam said, reassuring him. "Kreannot was here. You just missed him!"

Krass pinched her nose briefly. She flared her nostrils. "Smells much better now. We picked up an odor back there that was terrible."

Cringer guessed correctly that a Pelleezean had been in the woods. "A particularly pungent one," he added. "Tell us, Adam. What happened here tonight?"

As the three of them walked back slowly through the jungle,

Adam recounted everything. Or, almost everything. He held back the details of his final exchange with Kreannot. What Moss Man had said about home—his *true* home—had stuck with Adam. He knew what Krass would say if he mentioned it to her. She'd insist that the jungle was their home, that the tribe was their family.

But Adam wasn't sure he felt the same way.

When they returned to their hut, Adam fell asleep quickly, and the next day was a nonstop blur of dancing, eating, and games. Krass had a smile cemented on her face the entire time. Everyone in the tribe was celebrating, from cubs like Cormac, Cassius, Connor, and Cadum to the white-haired elders. Tiger Tribe musicians generally preferred drums, since cats struggled to play fiddles and harmonicas, but a few of the human members of the family were strumming string instruments, and the music was fantastic. Adam tried to enjoy himself. He ate until his stomach hurt, danced until his feet were numb, and even tried to beat the drums himself.

Yet he couldn't stop thinking about Moss Man.

He couldn't help but wonder why he'd made his choice.

As dusk settled, the party slowed, and the ceremony began with what Adam guessed were prayers, although they really just sounded like a series of low roars. At that point, he'd been living with the tigers for years, but he still couldn't quite speak cat. After a long sequence of solemn, serious growls, Cringer pounced onto the stage.

He called on Adam and Krass to join him. Krass raced up immediately. Adam followed. Everyone was watching them. He didn't like the attention. Facing the crowd, he held his arms behind his back, hiding his golden cuff as Cringer began to address the now quiet tribe.

"Greetings, family! I'm honored to sponsor these two today,"

Cringer intoned. "They might not have fur. Their teeth may be dull. They might walk on two legs instead of four, but in their hearts, Krass and Adam are both tigers!"

The crowd roared and cheered.

One of the tigers pounded on a drum with his paws.

"Today," Cringer continued, "they get their stripes!"

After the second round of applause and roars faded, Cringer nodded to them. "Who's first?"

Krass stepped forward eagerly. She was clutching something against her chest. Originally, she was going to give away her precious and ever-present helmet, but Cringer and the Tiger Tribe leaders decided that would be a really bad idea. Krass was always crashing into things. The helmet was essential protection. Now it looked to Adam like she was going to volunteer something else instead. What was it?

Holding one paw to Krass's shoulder, Cringer spoke more sacred words, and Krass repeated them in turn. Adam couldn't concentrate. He held his hands in front of him now and felt the golden cuff against his waist. If you weren't born in the tribe, you were supposed to give up something from your former life as proof of your allegiance. He was expected to give up the cuff. He'd already said that he would sacrifice it to show his loyalty to the tribe. But as he stood there on stage, listening to Krass reciting the ceremonial words with such heart and devotion, Adam wasn't sure he could actually do it. The cuff was the last remaining link to his old life—the forgotten, mysterious years before Cringer had found him abandoned in the jungle. Somehow, Adam knew, deep in his heart, that he still had a family out there somewhere. He believed he had a home. If he gave up this one reminder or piece of evidence, it would be like he was giving up on finding that home, and his family.

But no one gave up on a chance to join the tribe.

No one except Moss Man, apparently.

The ceremony had turned quiet.

Everyone was watching him, waiting. His turn to swear the oath to the tribe had come. Adam apologized, then stepped before Cringer. The wise tiger pronounced the sacred words. Adam repeated them automatically, without thought or feeling. He almost felt like he was in a trance. Still, he'd gotten through that part, at least. Now it was on to the next step.

Cringer turned back to Krass. "What do you volunteer as proof of your devotion, Krass?" the tiger asked.

Quietly, Krass held out a small photograph. The picture showed her smiling parents. Adam had seen this photo only once before. This was the only picture she still had of her mom and dad, who had perished in a terrible crash in the jungle. Krass looked like her father, Adam decided, and not just because her dad was wearing the gem-encrusted helmet she had now. Krass's father had insisted she wear the helmet before the accident, and it had probably saved her life, as she was the lone survivor.

Besides the helmet, the photo was her only remaining tie to them.

And now she was giving it to the tribe.

Tears pooled in her eyes.

But she handed the precious picture to Cringer.

The tiger nodded to Adam.

He looked down at the golden cuff.

Adam knew what he was supposed to do. The entire tribe was waiting for him to slip off the cuff. Krass elbowed him, urging him to get on with it. All he had to do was pass the golden cuff to Cringer.

Instead, Adam leaped off the stage and ran into his hut.

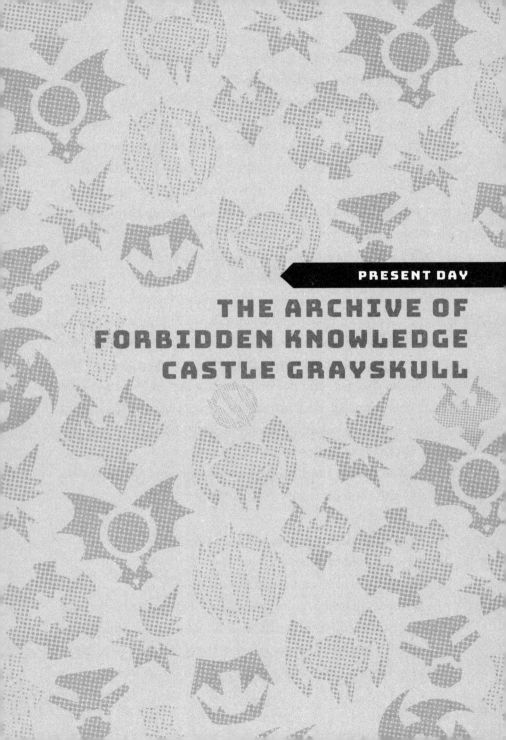

PRESENT DAY

THE ARCHIVE OF
FORBIDDEN KNOWLEDGE
CASTLE GRAYSKULL

8.

The four friends were still seated around the table in the library when Cringer, Adam, and Krass finished telling of their adventures with Odiphus and Moss Man. Two years had passed since the events. Adam and Krass had both grown, and changed, too. But the tension over Adam's decision hadn't faded. Krass snuck in a snide remark immediately. "Adam didn't even come out of his room until the next day," she added bitterly.

"That was also the last we heard of Kreannot, or smelled of the Pelleezeans, until this morning," Cringer said.

Duncan didn't help Adam's case. "We'll get to this Moss Man stuff in a minute," Duncan said, "but you bailed on the ceremony, Adam?"

"*And* on the tribe," Krass replied.

"You held onto that cuff, too, I see," Duncan added.

Adam crossed his arms on his chest. Yes, he'd refused to give up the cuff. But he was glad! The incantation that summoned the Power of Grayskull was magically inscribed in the band. If he hadn't been wearing the golden cuff when he first grasped the Sword of Power, he wouldn't have known to recite those words! If Adam had sacrificed it to the tribe, he never would have become He-Man. And if there was no He-Man, then no one would be around to stand up to Skeletor.

Had Krass forgotten that?

Adam felt a comforting paw on his shoulder, and Cringer spoke up for him. "Adam did what he felt he needed to do at the time."

"That doesn't make it right," Krass snapped.

Adam was so annoyed he nearly reached for his sword. Did He-Man and Ram Ma'am need to fight this one out?

He exhaled.

No—he knew that wouldn't be right. Body slamming one of your best friends out of frustration probably was no way to use the Power of Grayskull.

"I'm sorry," Adam said. "I've said it before and I'll say it again. I'm sorry."

"Yeah, well, good to see that you both let that one go," Duncan replied. "I was kind of hoping that talking it all out would clear the air, but that was an epic fail. So let's move on, okay? In case you forgot, we're supposed to be Masters of the Universe, stewards of Castle Grayskull and its powers, protectors of Eternia, and we need to find a way to stop this toxic plague. So let's forget about this cat initiation festival—no offense, Cringer—and focus on what you learned about Kreannot and the Pelleezeans and how that's going to help us solve this problem. These mossflowers Odiphus wanted obviously had some kind of power over the stench."

Adam exhaled, thankful that Duncan was changing the subject. "Right," he answered. "That's why Odiphus was looking for Kreannot in the first place."

"And you think the toxic air and that terrible perfume are one and the same?" Duncan asked.

"I'm certain of it," Cringer replied. "A tiger never forgets a scent, and that one was memorable."

"This is good!" Duncan exclaimed. He stood up and paced around the table. "Well, not *good*, exactly, but promising. I mean, in truth, it's terrible. But at least we have a potential fix. Based on what you learned that night, Adam, if the Pelleezean perfume is poison, then it sounds like the mossflower could be the antidote."

"Precisely," Cringer replied.

"Plus we know that he only blooms when he's happy," Adam said. "That's what he told me, anyway."

"We'll need something to spread the scent of the flowers," Krass added, "the way he did in the clearing."

"On a global scale," Cringer said.

"I could work on that," Duncan replied, "but we need the mossflowers first, and I still don't see how we're going to find our Moss Man. Your story didn't really help us there."

"No," Krass said, "but there are other stories we could learn from."

The three of them turned to look at her. Not one of them had a clue as to what she was talking about. Krass lifted her hands in the air, palms up, and motioned at their surroundings. "Duh! We're in a magical library! There has to be a book in here about his species."

Cringer dropped his huge head into his upturned paws. "How did I not think of that?"

Adam stared at the dozens of floating shelves. "This place is practically infinite. How are we supposed to find anything?"

He'd barely finished the question when one of the shelves drifted down to the floor. The image of a four-foot-tall scroll appeared on the side. Duncan bumped him out of the way. "Cool! A searchable catalog! There's no keyboard, though. Do you think it's voice activated?"

"Show us books on the Floranians," Cringer said.

The scroll blurred. When the type reformed, only a single title appeared.

"*A History of the Floranians*," Krass said, reading it aloud. "That's promising."

A quick summary of the book's contents appeared below the title. Based on the few lines of text, Adam guessed that this book would have everything they'd need to know and more about Kreannot and his species. There was a problem, though. A pretty enormous one, actually. "The book is marked as lost," Adam announced.

Krass was exasperated. "Lost? How does a magical library lose a book?"

Adam noticed a number in the far column. "Someone checked it out two hundred years ago and never returned it."

Cringer motioned toward the scroll with one of his metal claws. "Who is the author of the book?" he asked.

"Does it matter?" Duncan asked. "The book was written at least two hundred years ago. It's not like the author will be around to answer our questions."

"Do me the kindness of reading the name, please."

Adam glanced at the scroll. He shrugged. "Someone named Granamyr the Wise."

"Not a very humble name for an author," Duncan quipped.

Suddenly energized, Cringer slammed a paw down onto the table. "Duncan, is the *Wind Raider* ready for travel?"

"Sure," Duncan said. "Where are we going?"

"You're staying here," Cringer replied. "As long as Skeletor is out there, one of us needs to watch over Grayskull. Plus, you can start working on a way to spread the mossflower scent when we do find Kreannot. In the meantime, Adam, Krass, and I are going on a journey to the Ice Mountains."

Adam was stunned. The Ice Mountains were in the northern regions of Eternia, far beyond any cities. No one lived that far north! The air was frigid and cold and the desolate landscape was rumored to be a hideout for strange and dangerous creatures. Plus, it was really, really far away. "Why are we going to the Ice Mountains?" Adam asked. "That's practically the other side of the planet!"

"Because it's the home of Granamyr the Wise," Cringer replied. "The name is not a boast. Granamyr is believed to be one of the oldest, most knowledgeable beings in all of Eternia. Granamyr should be able to tell us what we need to know about Kreannot."

"Can't we just call or something?" Krass suggested. "I hate long flights."

Cringer shook his head. "Unfortunately, it's not that simple. You see, Granamyr doesn't particularly like humans, and I think we'll stand a better chance of asking for help in person—or in tiger, in my case. We need more information if we're going to find Kreannot, and right now, Granamyr the Wise is our best chance. And Adam?"

"Yes, Cringer?"

"Don't forget to bring your sword."

9.

The *Wind Raider* soared across Eternia. Duncan had given Cringer a few pointers on how to steer his precious ship—removing the metal claws was essential—but he hadn't modified the seats. The tiger had to stand on his hind legs, behind one of the pilot's chairs, and steer the controls that way. Still, Cringer was obviously proud of himself. Before the mishap with the *Eternia 2000*, he'd never flown an airship. Now he was practically a professional.

For the first part of the journey, Cringer flew above the clouds, careful to keep out of sight. But the lure of seeing so many new lands and territories proved too great, and the kids convinced the tiger to steer the *Wind Raider* closer to the ground. Adam, Krass, and the tiger himself gazed out through the windows at dense forests, wide and winding rivers, and countless small villages and farms.

At one point, Cringer slowed the ship and veered so close to a small coastal city that Adam could see the faces of people staring up at them. Part of him wanted to wave. Then he noticed two Red Legion Sky Sleds parked on a rooftop. The Red Legion was his father's troop of highly trained soldiers. Serving under General Dolos, they were some of the finest warriors in Eternos. Unfortunately, though, these once-loyal soldiers were now under Skeletor's sway. Through the power of Havoc, he controlled their minds, turning them into his brainless but still dangerous servants.

The last thing the Masters needed was to have Skeletor's minions following them. Adam urged Cringer to fly higher and faster.

Although she was excited for the adventure, Krass was getting increasingly impatient—she really did hate long trips. Cringer was oddly nervous, too. Why had he reminded Adam to bring the Sword of Power? Each of the Masters carried their power weapons everywhere. Krass rarely removed her helmet. Cringer had only slipped out of his claws to steer. And Adam always had the sword. When he slept, he slipped the sword beneath his mattress, with the handle sticking out, so he could grab it instantly if Skeletor snuck up on him in the middle of the night.

But why the urgency now? Why would he need a weapon if they were just going to ask some really old author a few questions?

Adam stood beside Cringer as the tiger steered the ship over tree-covered hills. Vast plains stretched out in front of them. The lands were neatly divided up into squares and rectangles, each one separated from its neighboring plots by roads and paths. Cringer uttered a low growl as they studied the scene, and Adam himself was shocked. The farms below them now weren't the bright green or radiant yellow of healthy lands.

Instead, everything had turned a dry and sandy brown.

When King Randor was on the throne, he might have helped. But Skeletor wouldn't care.

He'd probably let everyone down there starve.

The scene made Adam more determined than ever. No, he hadn't asked for the role of champion, but the inhabitants of Eternia needed someone to help them. Skeletor would let the planet turn into a wasteland.

And Adam was not going to let that happen.

The ship cruised over more dying farms, beyond the coast, and out over the radiant blue water of the Harmony Seas. Huge creatures swam in those depths. Adam had never been to the ocean before—or not as far as he could remember—and it was absolutely beautiful. He wanted Krass to see it, too, and turned to get her attention, but his friend was sound asleep at the back of the ship. Impatience was exhausting, apparently.

Inside the *Wind Raider*, the air turned cold. Adam started to shiver. Would it be weird to use the Sword of Power to warm up? He didn't remember ever being cold as He-Man. "Can we turn up the heat a little?" he asked.

"I'm perfectly warm," Cringer replied.

Yawning, Krass replied, "You're covered in fur." She crossed her arms over her chest and shivered. "I didn't realize I was that tired. It is pretty cold in here. Does that mean we're getting close?"

On the horizon, land appeared. White peaks loomed over the blue water. Adam pointed. "Is that where we're going? Are those the Ice Mountains?"

Krass laughed. "Do you think? They're literally covered in ice. They're not the Green Mountains. I have to ask, though. What sort of person would live up here?"

"Granamyr must really not like people," Adam added. "We must be hundreds of miles from the nearest city." Cringer said nothing; he remained solemn and serious. "What is it?" Adam asked. "What's wrong?"

Krass was first to notice the two figures perched on the mountainside. They could have been mistaken for sculptures, since they barely moved, and they were so far away that none of the three friends could make out exactly what they were seeing. But the sculptures seemed to have heads.

And the heads were turning toward the *Wind Raider*.

The strange figures shook themselves free of a coating of ice and snow and unfurled wide wings. Then they leaped from their positions and soared down the sides of the icy slopes toward the sea.

Cringer uttered a low growl. "I neglected to tell you that the Ice Mountains are not a particularly friendly place."

"So that's not a welcoming party?" Krass asked.

The creatures were speeding low over the water.

"Hey, Cringer?" Krass asked. "Are those dragons?"

"I'm afraid so," the tiger replied.

"Are you sure we need to see Granamyr?" Adam asked.

"We could always turn around," Krass suggested.

"No," Cringer replied. "We've come this far. We're not turning back now. But I do believe we should be ready to defend ourselves. Cubs?"

"Yes, Cringer?" Krass replied.

"I believe it's time to power up."

10.

The two dragons flew higher. One veered left, the other right, as the *Wind Raider* hurtled toward them through the icy air. Slowly, the creatures came into focus, and they definitely didn't look like a welcoming party. Their eyes were blazing red. Small tendrils of smoke trailed out of their mouths, and Adam thought he saw sharp teeth glimmering in the light. Fangs? Seriously? No one told him dragons had fangs, too. He reached over his shoulder and pulled out the Sword of Power. "Now?" he asked Cringer.

"Are you sure we want to call down the Power of Grayskull while we're inside the ship?" Krass asked. "I don't know if all that mystical lightning will be good for the *Wind Raider*. Plus, if we fry the electronics, Duncan's not here to fix things for us."

"Good point, Krass," Cringer noted. "Hold off for a moment."

The dragons were closer now, and each of the creatures was almost as large as the ship. The tiger turned the *Wind Raider* suddenly. Both Adam and Krass crashed into the left side of the cabin. Adam's shoulder ached. Krass laughed.

At the controls, Cringer radioed Duncan back at Castle Grayskull. Their friend sounded distracted, but he snapped to attention when Cringer asked if the *Wind Raider* was fireproof. "Sure," Duncan replied, his voice crackling. "Why?"

Relieved, Cringer dialed down the radio's volume.

One of the dragons swooped closer.

The smoke trailing from its mouth thickened.

The dragon bared its teeth and breathed out a stream of bright orange fire.

The *Wind Raider* dove, narrowly dodging the blast.

"How about now?" Adam asked. "Time for He-Man and Ram Ma'am?"

"I'll slam that featherless bird!" Krass shouted.

"Not yet!" Cringer insisted. "I'd prefer to avoid crashing into the sea. Let's set the ship down somewhere dry before we fight off these beasts."

"There!" Krass shouted, pointing ahead of them toward a wide plateau just beyond two of the icy peaks. Cringer steered the ship low, close to the sea surface, as the second dragon swooped around in front of them. The smoke leaking out of its mouth darkened.

The radio buzzed. "Umm, excuse me, what are you doing?" Duncan asked. "And why didn't you answer my question, Cringer?"

"We're busy trying to ditch some dragons," Adam answered. "Got any ideas?"

"Cringer?" Krass said, pointing at the approaching dragon, "I think this one's getting ready to—"

Before Krass could finish her sentence, the beast belched out a stream of fire, forcing Cringer to swerve once more out of the way. The *Wind Raider* skimmed the surface of the sea, nearly crashing into an oncoming wave, but the tiger steered it higher again just in time. Adam looked back, gripping his sword. The dragons were behind them now, flying side by side.

"Duncan?" Adam yelled. "Any suggestions?"

On the radio, Duncan's voice grew frantic with excitement. "I'm pretty sure most dragons need at least a minute to recharge their blasts," he said.

Incredulous, Adam asked, "How'd you know that?"

"I have a side interest in dragons. Fascinating science, you know? I've always wondered how their innards are insulated to protect them against—"

The inventor was cut off mid-sentence as Krass silenced the radio. Cringer stared at her, surprised. "What?" she replied. "He told us what we need to know, and you need to concentrate. If he's right, we have a minute before we need to power up and fight back."

The *Wind Raider* cleared the sea and accelerated straight up the ice-covered mountainside. Adam squeezed the hilt of the sword tighter. He could ask Cringer to open the rear bay of the ship, leap out, and ride the Sword of Power like a Sky Sled. He'd raced Stratos that way.[6] But he hadn't really mastered the technique yet.

---

6 The vain but impressive ruler of Avion, Stratos, narrowly defeated He-Man. But Adam earned his respect in the process—and his promise that Avion wouldn't blow Grayskull out of the sky.

"How much longer?" he called to Cringer.

"A few seconds, Adam!"

"The plateau's just ahead," Krass added.

The *Wind Raider* sped between the two peaks. Impatiently, Adam slammed the exit button on the side of the ship. The rear bay opened. The dragons were right behind the heroes now, their red eyes glaring. The smoke puffing out of their mouths was turning darker by the second. Their huge chests were filling with air. If the Masters didn't act fast, the two beasts might pump the entire cabin full of flames and sear the fur right off Cringer's back.

The *Wind Raider* straightened out and began to descend.

Her patience exhausted, Krass stood beside Adam. "I'm ready to ram!"

"NOW!" Cringer yelled.

As the two dragons swallowed deep breaths, preparing to unleash another round of fiery belches, Adam spread his feet, bent his knees, gripped the great sword with both hands, and pointed it toward the sky. Before he could say anything, though, Krass reached out and pushed down on his forearms, so the weapon aimed out the back of the ship, not up through the roof. She shrugged. "Just in case," she added.

"Good idea," Adam conceded. He breathed in through his nose, tensed his still-small muscles, and glanced at his friend beside him. Krass was crouched low, her feet staggered. Together, they proclaimed, "BY THE POWER OF GRAYSKULL!"

The moment they spoke the words, the ship, the dragons, and the Ice Mountains vanished. The sky crackled with mystical lightning as power flooded into Adam's rapidly growing frame. Within seconds, the transformation was complete, and he felt the incomparable strength of Grayskull pulsing in every muscle. Adam extended his sword and added, "I HAVE THE POWER!"

Flashes of energy sparked off his friend as Krass turned into the unstoppable Ram Ma'am. The huge crystals that lined the front of her upgraded helmet, the Helm of Destruction, glowed brightly. Her rocket-powered helmet and armored boots were already firing up as she, too, declared, "I HAVE THE POWER!"

The dragons' eyes grew wide with shock as the beasts stared back at He-Man and Ram Ma'am.

"No Battle Cat?" Rammy called back to Cringer.

"I'm too large as Battle Cat," the tiger explained. "I fear I'd crush Duncan's precious ship from the inside out. I'll join you after I land. Now hurry up!"

The shocked dragons drifted back at first, then refocused, flying closer. One of them reared back, as if ready to fire, when Ram Ma'am elbowed her friend. "How's that throwing arm, He-Man?" she asked.

"You're not going to catapult yourself?"

"Are you really passing up a chance to toss your best friend?"

No. Absolutely not. He-Man grabbed Ram Ma'am by the back of her armored suit, spun around once to build momentum, and hurled her out of the back of the *Wind Raider* at the first dragon. The beast was ready to fire when Rammy smashed into its stomach, and the pair of them crashed down onto the icy plateau.

The second dragon pushed forward as if it were ready to fly straight into the ship. He-Man crouched, sprinted three steps, and launched himself into the frigid air. The surprised dragon tried to dodge the huge champion, but He-Man reached out with his free hand and grabbed the end of one of its wings.

Desperate, the dragon shot a stream of fire, but it fizzled on contact with the Sword of Power. Then dragon and hero tumbled down from the sky and smashed onto the ice. Huge cracks spread in every direction.

He-Man leaped to his feet.

Dazed, the dragon unfurled its wings, staggering away.

The beast didn't look like a monster. Not up close, anyway. He-Man had a feeling the dragon might be a kid. Still, even if his instincts were accurate, this monster had tried to fry their ship. He-Man couldn't just let it free. He crouched into fighting position, glowering as he held the sword. The glower didn't feel quite right, though. He tried to lift his upper lip at one side, thinking a sneer might be more menacing.

The dragon tilted its head and snout. "What are you doing?"

The voice of the creature confirmed his suspicion. If He-Man had to guess, this dragon wasn't much older than Adam and Krass. And the fact that the beast found both his glower and his sneer unimpressive was a little disappointing. He'd have to work on that before he faced Skeletor and the Dark Masters again. "At first I was glowering," He-Man answered. "But this is my menacing sneer."

"It's not working," the dragon replied, "and you should probably be less worried about your expression and more about my buddy."

"Your buddy?"

He-Man had barely finished his question when he felt powerful talons dig into his shoulders. A shadow covered him. His feet rose off the ice, and he looked up to see the second dragon flying him up into the sky.

One swing of his sword was all he needed.

The dragon roared as He-Man smacked the flat end of the blade against its leathery stomach. The champion dropped to the ice as the beast swooped away. The other dragon beat its wings, and the pair of them circled the plateau.

A few hundred yards away, Rammy fired energy bands from her armored hips, slingshotted herself toward He-Man, then screeched to a stop beside him. Meanwhile, Cringer leaped out of the *Wind Raider.* He slipped his paws into his metal claws, raced away from the ship, and declared, "BY THE POWER OF GRAYSKULL . . . I HAVE THE POWER!"

The old tiger grew into a fearsome beast several times his normal size. His red armored headpiece gleamed. The simple metal claws Duncan had made him powered up into the radiant Claws of the Wild, and his roar was loud enough to shake the icy ground.

As Battle Cat raced toward Adam and Ram Ma'am, a strange beam of blue light shot out of the sky, striking the ship.

Instantly, the *Wind Raider* was encased in thick blue ice.

He-Man winced. Duncan wasn't going to like that.

The pair of dragons weren't the source of the magical beam—the light was coming from what looked like an open window, halfway up an icy mountain at the far side of the plateau.

"That's our ride!" Rammy yelled.

"Who did that?" He-Man asked.

As the dragons circled above them, Battle Cat growled. "We'll worry about the *Wind Raider* later. I neglected to tell you this earlier, but Granamyr the Wise is also a sorcerer. A powerful one, at that." He eyed the icy mountain. The window-like opening was one of a dozen spread up and down the frozen face. "And I suspect we've found our sorcerer's lair."

"Well, it doesn't seem like Granamyr wants any visitors," Rammy replied. "What now?"

One of the dragons was turning and aiming for the trio of friends.

The dragon drew in a huge breath of air, ready to blast them with fire.

He-Man charged forward bravely.

Before he came within striking distance of the dragon, a spinning ball of light and energy shot through the air and smashed into the creature. The blur and the dragon both crashed into the ice below. Then the glowing sphere slowed. Rammy rolled to a stop, jumped up, and raced back to her friends, zooming across the plateau. "I think I'm even faster on the ice!" she said.

Now she stood shoulder to shoulder with He-Man.

Or shoulder to stomach, really.

He-Man was as tall as a giant.

Battle Cat roared, and the dragons knew better than to challenge the three Masters. The two winged beasts escaped into the air.

"Now what?" Rammy asked.

He-Man studied their surroundings. The high icy wall, inlaid with windows, leaned back at an angle that nearly matched the mountain's slope, and its sides glimmered in the sunlight. Although it looked like a castle of some kind, there was no gate or entry at the bottom. He-Man was about to ask for ideas on how to get inside when Rammy pointed up toward the top. The dragons were flying to a stone perch that extended out from a tall opening.

"Where are they going?" Rammy asked.

"What is that place?" He-Man added.

"If I had to guess," Battle Cat answered, "that would be Grana-myr's castle."

"Weird house," Rammy noted. "I guess the front door makes sense if you can fly, but if I was this Granamyr guy, I'd add a normal one down here at ground level, too."

"Yes, well, Granamyr isn't exactly a guy."

"What do you mean?"

The two sentries disappeared into the opening.

Seconds later, a huge burst of flame exploded out from inside the castle.

Battle Cat dug in his Grayskull-strengthened claws.

"Is there something else you forgot to tell us?" He-Man asked.

"Yes," Battle Cat confessed. "First of all, Granamyr is female."

"Really?" He-Man asked, surprised.

"Should that matter?" Rammy countered.

No, He-Man realized. Not at all.

"And she isn't merely a sorcerer," Cringer added. "She is also one of the most powerful dragons in the history of Eternia."

11.

The Masters eyed the sheer wall of rock and ice.

The entrance was as high off the ground as a small mountain peak. But He-Man had leaped at least that high in the past. He could try again, but he didn't want to leave his friends behind. They were in this together. "Can you two get up there without the ship?" he asked.

Battle Cat was eyeing a crag in the mountain off to their right. His Claws of the Wild extended, digging into the ice. "Don't insult me," the tiger replied.

Rammy? She winked, then fired two energetic cables from her suit, anchoring them in the ice, and pulled herself back as far as she could. "Last one up's a rotten navit!"

Sparks flew in all directions as Ram Ma'am launched forward.

A spinning, whirling ball of light with He-Man's best friend inside screamed across the ice and up the mountainside.

Battle Cat laughed, then leaped toward the crag.

He-Man really didn't want to be a rotten navit.

They stunk almost as bad as Pelleezean perfume.

There was only one thing to do now.

He raced forward as fast as he could, took several small jumps, then planted both of his feet on the frozen ground and pushed off with all his might. Immediately, he soared as if he'd been shot out of a cannon. The icy air on his face renewed his vigor, and he landed with a thud on the balcony high above. Rammy had already zoomed past him. He-Man worried she was going to launch herself right over the top of the peak and out into the sea beyond. Then, inches from the top of the mountain, she slowed to a stop and began to drop back down. He-Man reached out and grabbed her, yanking her over onto the safety of the balcony as Battle Cat jumped into place beside them.

The fierce tiger roared.

Rammy was beaming. "That was fun!"

At the far side of the balcony stood the door to a cavernous room. Gray and white smoke billowed out. The winged sentries that had attacked the *Wind Raider* were nowhere in sight. The scene was eerily calm.

He-Man didn't like it at all.

Then the balcony shook.

Seconds later it rumbled again.

Protectively, He-Man stepped out in front of his friends. Neither of them had any interest in cowering behind the champion, however. As He-Man edged forward, Rammy and Battle Cat moved with him.

Again and again the ground shook.

"Is that an earthquake?" Rammy asked.

"That's no earthquake," Battle Cat answered. "I fear those are footsteps."

The sound stopped.

Seconds passed in tense silence.

An intermittent breeze blew from inside the cave.

Yet these were no gusts of wind.

They were the breaths of an enormous beast.

In the darkness of the doorway, a shape took form. A yellow light brightened, and the eye of a dragon appeared in the darkness.

"She's bigger than I thought," He-Man said.

"Much bigger," Rammy added. "One good thing, though."

"What's that?" Battle Cat asked.

"Looks like she's too big to squeeze through that front door," Rammy said. "So maybe we can just ask for her help from out here?"

He-Man patted his huge chest and cleared his throat. How did one address an ancient dragon sorcerer? "Excuse us, winged wise one—"

"SILENCE!" the dragon growled.

Next they heard a kind of muttering, and the door before them began to change. The stone frame started to wobble. Ripples passed through the rock and ice like waves through water, and the door began to grow. Within seconds, it had expanded to twice its former size, and it kept growing larger and larger.

Finally, Granamyr stepped forward into the icy blue light of day.

The dragon sorcerer looked like her two smaller sentries, only four or five times as large. Her purple skin was ridged, wrinkled, and leathery. Her huge yellow eyes looked down at them above a pair of giant, smoking nostrils. Fangs jutted out of a mouth that looked large enough to swallow the *Wind Raider*, and a jaw strong enough to crush it. The dragon's legs were thick and powerful, her arms thin but strong. And her belly was so vast and cavernous that He-Man wondered if this dragon snacked on passing ships. Granamyr was undoubtedly fearsome. But she didn't look like she worked out that much.

Once she was clear of the doorway, the dragon reared back and stood to her full height. "Who dares invade my territory?"

He-Man remained silent. Rammy and Battle Cat, too.

The dragon repeated her question.

None of the Masters said a word.

Granamyr puffed out a cloud of smoke in frustration. Her voice had lost some of its power when she asked, "Why aren't you speaking?"

"You told us to be silent," He-Man noted.

"You literally yelled 'SILENCE,'" Krass added.

"It was quite convincing," said Battle Cat.

"Yes, well, now you can speak. Who are you and what are you doing at the door to my castle?"

He-Man took a deep breath and tried to stand taller. "We are the Masters of the Universe," he said, "and we need your help."

The dragon paused. She eyed He-Man's sword. And then she began to laugh. "You might be the Masters of the Universe, but I am the master of the Ice Mountains, and I'd like you to leave."

"No," Rammy answered.

"Excuse me?"

"I said, NO. We're not leaving here until you at least hear what we've come to say."

"You will leave," the dragon replied, "when I want you to leave."

Granamyr sucked in a huge breath of air, one that expanded her chest to almost twice its previous size.

"Run!" Battle Cat roared. "Take cover!"

Rammy rushed to the right. Battle Cat dashed left. But He-Man did not move. He bent his knees, raised the Sword of Power, and held his ground as a river of flame shot toward him from the great dragon's mouth.

12.

The Sword of Power did not come with an instruction manual, so it was no small risk the champion took when he stood in the path of that flame. He'd blocked a smaller blast, but no one had actually informed him that the blade could protect him against the incinerating breath of a far more powerful dragon. And yet it worked.

As He-Man held the sword upright and leaned his right shoulder forward, the flames bent around him like a river splitting in the path of a huge boulder. Sweat was bursting out of his pores. His face and right arm were burning. His legs, too. But he was alive.

No—he was more than alive.

He felt even stronger.

The power within him seemed to grow, as if it was intensifying to meet the challenge of the dragon. The normally invisible tattoos on his arm, the sigils of his power, began to glow with radiant golden light. The same thing happened when he called on his Lightning Strike attack, too. He-Man kind of wished they shined all the time. Adam never would've guessed he'd be into tattoos, but these magical Grayskull ones were awesome.

He pressed forward, step by step.

He hoped Battle Cat and Rammy were safe—he couldn't hear or see them. The dragon seemed to be focusing all her fiery power on him. The beast had a serious set of lungs, too, because she still hadn't stopped for another breath of air.

The fire wasn't slowing or weakening.

He-Man didn't want to destroy the dragon. They'd come all this way to talk, not fight. But he needed to convince the beast that he was someone worthy of her attention, not her destructive breath. Lowering his shoulder, He-Man moved forward one difficult step at a time.

The fire grew hotter and hotter.

His face was soaked with sweat.

He had to put a stop to this attack.

Crouching low, He-Man summoned all his strength and leaped forward into the raging flame.

The fire flowed around him, and then he was clear of the dragon's breath, rolling to the ground at Granamyr's leathery, clawed feet. The flame was above his head now, striking the ground behind him, where he'd stood only seconds before, and the preoccupied dragon didn't even see him.

The ancient sorcerer was too busy breathing fire to notice.

He-Man looked up at the beast's huge, heaving stomach. He

tossed the sword from right hand to left. Then he jumped, tightened his fist, and punched the dragon cleanly in the gut.

The flame sputtered.

Granamyr gasped.

She coughed out puffs of white smoke and stumbled backward. Out of the darkness of the castle, two smaller dragons flew around her and into the air behind He-Man. Another pair followed. The sentries—He-Man recognized them from the fight on the plateau—were next. As the air cleared, Battle Cat and Rammy hurried to He-Man's side. A final dragon swooped out of the darkness. Yet this one flew erratically, dropping one second, flapping its wings to rise up the next, as if it were still learning how to fly.

"What now?" Battle Cat asked.

"More ramming?"

"No," He-Man replied. "We came here to talk."

The dragon sorcerer stopped backing up. The puffs of smoke ceased. She breathed in deeply, as if clearing her lungs, and stood taller. One at a time, the circling dragons swooped down and landed deftly beside her. All except the last one—the struggling dragon timed its final circle wrong and slammed straight into the icy wall. With its wings spread out wide, the dragon clawed at the ice with its feet, but slipped down before it could stop its slide and crashed to the floor.

"She's so embarrassing," one of the dragons muttered.

"She's your sister!" Granamyr roared, "and in a century or two she'll be more powerful than the lot of you put together!"

The fallen dragon stood, shook out her wings, and slumped over to the others, embarrassed. The beasts stood at Granamyr's side.

The tallest one barely reached the top of her huge stomach. The smallest—the girl—was still larger than He-Man. And all of them had their chests puffed up, as if they were ready to unleash another round of fiery blasts as soon as Granamyr gave the order.

"We're not here to fight!" He-Man insisted. "I'm He-Man. These are my friends Battle Cat and Ram Ma'am."

"We merely have questions," Battle Cat said.

The huge gemstone in Rammy's Helm of Destruction sparked. "But we'll fight if we have to," she said.

"Rammy!" Battle Cat roared. "That's not helpful."

"I appreciate your honesty, young lady," Granamyr replied. "But I will warn you that my children and I will fight to the death to defend our home, if necessary."

"I understand," He-Man replied. "We don't mean to threaten you. We know the importance of defending one's home."

Ram Ma'am sneered. "Oh, do we, He-Man?"

Adam briefly closed his eyes and sighed with frustration. She was back on the Tiger Tribe thing *again*? "Not now, Rammy."

"Skeletor could be invading our jungle right now—"

"Skeletor?" Granamyr interrupted. "Is this the new tyrant who rules the world of men?"

"And women," Krass added.

"Yes," Battle Cat answered. "He sits on the throne in Eternos. He wants to turn all of Eternia into a wasteland."

"But he's not the reason we're here, Granamyr," He-Man said. "We're not here to fight, either. We need your help."

"If you're not here to fight, then why do you brandish that sword?"

He-Man looked down at the Sword of Power. What if he sheathed his weapon? What if he powered down to show Granamyr that they didn't mean to be a threat? He looked to Battle Cat, who shook his enormous head, silently guessing what He-Man was thinking. If he powered down, he'd transform back into a sixteen-year-old kid. A scrawny teenager who definitely wouldn't be able to withstand the deadly breath of an ancient dragon.

"Please," Battle Cat interjected. "We ask only for information. According to legend, you are one of the oldest creatures in Eternia—"

"Not even close!" Granamyr protested. "There's at least one tree who has me beat by a few hundred years. I've heard of a mushroom who might be four million years old, too. She's very private, though, and lives underground. Then there are the Floranians, too. They are at least . . . what?"

The eyes of the three Masters widened collectively at the mention of the Floranians. "That's why we're here," He-Man said. "We're hoping to learn more about the Floranians. We need to find one in particular . . . most Eternians call him Moss Man, even though his real name is Kreannot . . . and we hoped you might be able to help."

"We wanted to read your book—"

"My book?" Now Granamyr stood even taller. She tilted her huge head to one side and leaned forward, lowering her voice. "You know of my book?"

"Yes," Rammy answered. "It was supposed to be in the library at Grayskull, but it was missing."

"Now that is a *true* tragedy," Granamyr replied.

He-Man leaned forward. "I'm sorry to press, but do you know how we might be able to find this Floranian we're looking for?"

"She knows everything," the youngest dragon chirped in. "She's the wisest being in all of Eternia."

Before the young dragon could even finish her sentence, Granamyr spat a fireball at her feet. The little dragon leaped backward and tripped over her wings. "Quiet," Granamyr snapped.

She turned back to the Masters and studied them through narrowed eyes.

Instinctively, He-Man gripped the Sword of Power, ready to protect his friends if the dragon decided to spit a fireball in their direction, too.

Granamyr noticed the champion tightening his fists. Her long mouth curled into an angry scowl. "Leave my island now," she pronounced. "I decided long ago that I would no longer involve myself in the affairs of humans. I don't trust men." She turned toward Rammy. "Nor women."

Rammy crouched into a fighting stance. The ram stone in her helmet began roiling with energy. Sparks flew out of her rocket-powered boots.

Battle Cat extended his Grayskull-powered Claws of the Wild, and they crackled with energy and power.

The two Masters looked ready to wrestle the answers out of the dragon.

But He-Man guessed another battle wasn't going to get them anywhere.

He had to show this ancient being that he was telling the truth.

Slowly, with his eyes locked on those of Granamyr, He-Man lowered the Sword of Power to the ground at the beast's feet. Rammy tried to stop him. Battle Cat, too. But He-Man was determined, and the champion backed away from the tempestuous sorcerer.

Granamyr did not move toward the sword.

Neither did any of her dragon descendants.

Instead, they watched in wonder as He-Man transformed.

This part, for Adam, was still super weird, in part because it was instantaneous. In a flash, his huge arms shortened and shriveled. His legs, too. The giant, powerful muscles that stretched across his chest and popped out of his back all but disappeared. His rib cage shrank, and he turned from a massive warrior back into a scrawny teen.

Standing before the dragon, Adam shrugged.

The suspicious glare on Granamyr's face relaxed.

Now the dragon regarded him with awe.

"You said you don't trust men or women," Adam replied. "Well, I'm not a man. I'm a kid, and I need your help."

13.

When the three Masters had flown down from Avion earlier that morning, they hadn't really thought about what they'd eat or drink on their journey. But if you had asked them to guess, not a single one of the heroes would have imagined they'd be sitting down for tea with the most powerful dragon in Eternia. Granamyr, as it turned out, had no interest in fighting. All she wanted was to keep her family of firebreathers safe from harm.

Once He-Man laid down his sword and transformed into Adam, her mood changed completely. Instead of attacking the suddenly weakened champion, she'd turned into a most gracious host and invited the three Masters inside for a late-morning snack. Now the four of them sat around a large stone table as the younger dragons flitted about, delivering cookies, cakes, and pots of absolutely scalding tea. Both Battle Cat and Ram Ma'am had powered down as well, reverting to their usual forms. Granamyr sat on a high-backed chair, but the three friends were too small for the remaining seats. The dragons had flown Krass and Adam up to the table's edge, where they sat with their legs crossed before mugs as big as bathtubs. Cringer had leaped up on his own—he grumbled that he wasn't so old that he couldn't jump anymore.

The table was set with the largest desserts any of them had ever seen. A square of lemon cake stood as high as Adam's chest. The layer of vanilla frosting on top was as thick as the biggest books in Grayskull's library. And the cookies and tea biscuits were enormous, too. Krass actually lay down flat on the table beside one of the chocolate cookies to prove that it was as wide as she was tall. Transforming into He-Man tended to stoke Adam's appetite, and he nearly ate half the giant piece of cake himself.

Normally, Cringer wasn't one for sweets, but not even the tiger could resist swiping a paw through some of the frosting for a taste test. When he finished licking his lips and cleaning his metallic claws, he addressed their host. "I should say again that we are sorry for charging into your land unannounced, Granamyr," the tiger said, "but this is an emergency."

Two dragons flew over to the table carrying another teapot. They hovered skillfully above the table, then tipped it forward, pouring a dark, steaming brew into Granamyr's cup. After her first careful sip, the dragon placed her cup down and asked Cringer to tell him about the emergency. As Krass and Adam worked through the giant desserts, the tiger told Granamyr everything they knew about the powerful Pelleezean odor that was ruining farms across Eternia, including the role of the *Eternia 2000*, their fear that

Skeletor could use the stench to his advantage, and their history with Odiphus and the legendary Moss Man.

When Cringer finished, Granamyr sat back and sighed.

Adam swallowed down his last bite of cake.

Krass belched. "Excuse me," she apologized.

"That's perfectly excusable," Granamyr replied. Then she turned to one side and burped out a ball of flame. "It's the sign of a good snack in dragon culture. Now, my friends, as for your quest, I will tell you what I know. First of all, not every mossflower is the same. In my younger days, I knew a very, very loquacious tree—"

"Loquacious?" Adam asked.

"Verbose, talkative, chatty," Granamyr explained. "If you happened to smell one of his flowers, you wouldn't stop talking for hours. It was funny for some, but terrible for others. One of my friends at the time was human, and after he accidentally inhaled the perfume of one of these mossflowers, he told his wife all his deepest, darkest secrets. She kicked him out of their house—a well-deserved punishment—and he had to live with us dragons for a while."

"Wow. What happened to him?"

"I don't know. He's been dead for a millennium. You humans don't live very long. As I was saying, though, each mossflower is unique. You think this particular Floranian's flower could counteract the toxic gas?"

"We know it," Adam said. "We saw it in action. We just need to find him and convince him to help us."

"Any ideas about how we might do that?" Krass asked.

Granamyr leaned back and squinted at the ceiling. "Most Floranians do not move very often. They prefer to establish roots. When they find a suitable and pleasant home, they stay there, and the trees and plant life around them bloom. Their own mossflowers, too. There is no grove quite so beautiful as one inhabited by one of these beings."

"I don't think Kreannot is like the others," Adam said. "From what we know, he's always moving."

"Interesting," Granamyr replied. "I wonder—what if it isn't finding a home that causes this Kreannot friend of yours to bloom? What if it's movement? The other Floranians are happiest when they settle down and stretch their roots. What if he's happiest when he's traveling Eternia?"

Adam looked to Cringer and Krass. "That makes sense, I guess, but I still don't see how it would help us find him."

Granamyr grumbled. She closed her eyes. Krass started to say something, but Cringer motioned for her to be quiet. The dragon was thinking. Finally, Granamyr opened her eyes and stared at the ceiling. "If he blooms when he's happy, and he's happiest when traveling, and his mossflowers are truly as powerful as you say, then you should be able to see a change in the lands he has ventured through."

"Wait . . . what do you mean?" Adam asked.

"If this toxic wind has settled in one region, and your Moss Man travels through happily, you should see the changes reversed. The ruined lands should turn fertile and vibrant again."

Adam paused, thinking.

Granamyr's logic made perfect sense.

They had to tell Duncan. "We have to go!" he said.

Suddenly, Cringer growled and turned in the direction of the exit.

"What is it?" Krass asked.

The tiger snarled. "Does anyone else smell that?"

Both Krass and Adam shrugged. Granamyr, too. "Don't tell anyone, but dragons have a terrible sense of smell," she confessed. "That's what happens when you singe the inside of your nose on a regular basis."

"What sort of smell? Is it Pelleezean?" Krass asked.

"No," Cringer replied, lowering his voice. "It smells like danger."

14.

As Granamyr wondered aloud what, exactly, danger might smell like, the young dragons flew up a long, winding ramp and out through the towering front door. Adam, Krass, and Cringer hurried behind, and the ground below them shook as a furious Granamyr stomped at their heels. Out on the balcony, Adam had to squint as his eyes adjusted to the cold bright light, but soon the source of Cringer's concern was clear enough.

A swarm of eight Red Legion Sky Sleds hovered in the distance.

"Not again," Cringer replied.

"Friends of yours?" Granamyr asked.

Adam sneered at the sight of the hovercrafts. Each of the Sky Sleds had four laser cannons glowing green with Havoc. "They're members of the Red Legion, sworn to protect Eternos," he explained, "but they're being controlled by Skeletor."

"Well, they're not welcome here," Granamyr announced.

"We can't hurt them," Cringer explained. "The soldiers are innocent. They don't know what they're doing."

"How did they even find us?" Krass asked.

"We flew too close to that city," Adam recalled. "They must have tracked us." He faced the dragon. "This is our fault, Granamyr. We brought this chaos to your home. We'll take care of it for you."

A confident smile flashed on his face as Adam extended his sword and intoned, "BY THE POWER OF GRAYSKULL . . ."

This time, Krass didn't feel like waiting for Adam to finish his show. "BY THE POWER OF GRAYSKULL," she repeated, and the energy coursed through her helmet and body. Cringer followed next, his power claws igniting, and then all three Masters declared, "WE HAVE THE POWER!"

Adam rolled his suddenly huge shoulders and tightened into a fighting stance as He-Man. With a powerful roar, Battle Cat leaped into place beside him, and Rammy crouched next to the giant armored tiger, powered up and ready to demolish whatever stood in her path.

The Sky Sleds aimed blasts of devastating Havoc at the Masters.

He-Man rapidly swung the Sword of Power, smashing each of the green, laser-like blasts back into the cloudless sky.

Adam had no intention of knocking the sleds down with his return shots, but the vehicles swerved and regrouped anyway.

"How do you propose to stop them if you can't hurt them?" Granamyr asked.

The jets at the back of Rammy's Helm of Destruction were spitting out blasts of energy. He-Man could see she was growing more impatient by the second. Then her eyes widened. She looked back and forth between the Red Legion Sky Sleds and the dragons. Finally, she smiled. "Hey, Granamyr? Would you mind if I borrowed a few of your kids—"

"Grandkids, actually," the dragon corrected her.

"Okay . . . would you mind if I borrowed a few of your grandkids for a game of catch?"

The dragon was too perplexed to answer, and Rammy didn't wait for her reply anyway. She didn't wait for approval from He-Man or Battle Cat, either. Instead, she blasted herself straight at the nearest Havoc-powered hovercraft. He-Man watched as a whirling, Ram Ma'am–sized ball of energy streaked forward and crashed into the side of the Sky Sled. For a moment, He-Man panicked as the mind-controlled Red Legion pilot tumbled sideways out of the vehicle. The soldier was plummeting toward the plateau below when one of the dragons swooped down, snatched him by the back of his armored uniform, and flew him over to the balcony.

Right.

A game of catch.

Rammy-style.

Down below, Ram Ma'am spun to a stop on the ice, then turned and prepared to rocket herself at the next vehicle.

"Fabulous!" Granamyr shouted. "We don't get much entertainment here in the Ice Mountains. Self-imposed exile is so boring."

The first dragon dropped the Red Legion soldier onto the balcony.

The mind-controlled minion of Skeletor started to reach for a weapon.

Battle Cat pounced, digging his claws into the balcony floor and roaring with so much force that the soldier cowered and held up his hands. Not even the power of Havoc could convince him to challenge Battle Cat. "I'll guard the soldiers, He-Man," the tiger decided. "You help Ram Ma'am."

The remaining Sky Sleds fired another volley of Havoc blasts, but He-Man swatted them away. Then, spotting two of the vehicles flying close together, he leaped high into the air, soared down, and grabbed one with each hand. The pilots tried to steer away, but He-Man slammed the two Sky Sleds together. A plume of Havoc erupted from the engines, and the soldiers bailed off the sides. Once again, the dragons soared in before the pilots hit the ground and flew the prisoners over to Battle Cat.

He-Man landed with a crash on the icy plateau.

Above him, Rammy was bouncing between Sky Sleds.

She took out four of them, careening from ship to ship.

Now only a single Sky Sled remained. And this final ship was turning toward He-Man, aiming its Havoc-fueled cannons right at him. He didn't see the blast soon enough to knock it away, and he barely leaped aside in time to avoid the blow. And yes, he knew it wasn't the pilot's fault. He knew the soldier had Havoc on the brain. But He-Man still wanted to teach the soldier a lesson. He crouched, ready to hurl himself straight at the Sky Sled, when he caught one of the strangest sights he'd ever seen out of the corner of his eye.

The enormous, aged dragon known as Granamyr the Wise was flying just above the remaining Sky Sled. In her huge, leathery feet, she held Battle Cat. The tiger was almost as long as she was tall, and the purple glow around the cat suggested that Granamyr was using a bit of sorcery to help with the flight. As the pair approached, Granamyr flung the tiger forward. Battle Cat backflipped, then dropped down onto the Sky Sled from behind, swiping at the clueless pilot's hovercraft with his sparkling yellow claws.

The Sky Sled spun into several backflips of its own.

The pilot was hurled out of his seat.

This time, though, it looked like no one was around to grab him.

The green-eyed, Havoc-controlled guard was going to crash.

He-Man started to race across the ice, hoping to break the soldier's fall, when the youngest dragon swooped in and snagged him by the ankles. The dragon briefly lost her grip. The soldier screamed as he started to drop again, but she grabbed him once more before he hit the ice.

"Sorry, that was an accident!" the young dragon replied.

As the remaining dragons guarded the captured soldiers on the balcony above, Rammy raced back to meet Battle Cat, He-Man, and Granamyr. Gloating, she turned to He-Man. "Not that I was keeping score or anything," she began, "but I did beat you five to two."

"I'd say that's less of a victory than an annihilation," Granamyr remarked.

The lone soldier on the plateau stumbled to one side, then the other, before dropping to the ice. Battle Cat rushed to him. He leaned in close to the fallen pilot, then looked up at his friends. "He merely fainted," the tiger said. "He'll be fine."

He-Man turned to the dragon. "What should we do with him and the others, Granamyr?"

The ancient sorcerer gazed sympathetically at the fallen soldier. "I suppose they can stay here for now. I'll see if I can find a spell to counter Skeletor's work and free their minds. While we're on the subject of spells, though, I confess that I'm a little out of practice." The dragon turned toward the ice-encased *Wind Raider.* "I don't exactly recall how to free your ship."

The young dragon eagerly volunteered to help, insisting that she had a solution. Without waiting for approval, she flew over to the magically frozen ship and breathed out a gust of bright orange flame. The ice melted instantly. That part was great. The unfortunate piece? She also charred one of the wings.

"Duncan's going to be furious," He-Man muttered.

The dragon winced. "Sorry! I'm still practicing."

Battle Cat motioned to the fallen soldier on the ice, and the prisoners up on the balcony. "Are you sure we can't help, Granamyr?" he asked.

"Go," the dragon replied. "Find your Moss Man!"

15.

The *Wind Raider* cruised south. Cringer had switched to auto-pilot, and each of the heroes relaxed as the ship soared over the sea. Adam was still adjusting to his suddenly small body. The switch back was always odd. It happened so quickly, and afterward Adam sometimes found himself ducking or leaning through doorways unnecessarily. His jaw felt strange, too, once it shrank down to half its former size, and while he missed He-Man's muscles, the ship did feel roomier without them. Adam was way more comfortable in his scrawny teenage form. He kicked back in one of the pilot's seats, gazing out at the surrounding water. A quick nap would be ideal. He hadn't been sleeping all that much since becoming the most powerful man in the universe. The new responsibilities had a way of keeping him up at night.

The truth was that he couldn't really relax, no matter how comfortable the seats. Especially now that Skeletor's mind-controlled Red Legion soldiers had tracked them. Adam guessed they'd reported back to the evil tyrant before flying to the Ice Mountains, too. Plus, Skeletor himself had a weird way of sensing whenever Adam and his friends called on the Power of Grayskull. The tyrant would be wondering what they were up to, and Adam needed to find out what his boneheaded uncle was doing, too.

Cringer summoned Duncan on the holographic projector. Their friend was still inside Grayskull's archive. In a rush, Adam and Krass reviewed what they'd learned. The digital projection of Duncan leaned to one side; he pointed to the control panel behind Cringer. "Why does that screen say there's fire damage to the starboard wing?"

Reaching back, Cringer swiped a paw at the dashboard, shutting off the display. "Never mind that, Duncan. How do we find Kreannot?"

"Just don't break my ship, okay? Please?" Duncan replied. "As for finding Kreannot, our air sensors are covering most of the planet, so we have a pretty clear picture of where the toxic stench is blowing. The bad news? The gas is everywhere."

"Okay," Adam began, "and the good news?"

"Granamyr's idea was brilliant," Duncan said. "I think I can use our artificial noses to track Kreannot."

"How?" Adam asked.

Krass clapped her hands. "I know!"

"You know what?"

She pointed to Duncan. "I know what you're thinking! If the toxins are pretty much everywhere, and Kreannot's mossflower blooms when he's on the move . . ."

"Then we should also see a change in the air wherever he has traveled," Duncan said, finishing her thought. "So, if we compare the early readings from the sensors with the data they're getting now, we might be able to identify a trail along which the toxic gas has been neutralized."

"And if we find the trail . . ."

"Then we find our Floranian nearby."

Cringer growled with approval. "What do you need to get this done, my ingenious friend?"

The engineer didn't answer. With the other Masters watching him remotely, Duncan set to work reprogramming the display. As he did so, he explained that any stretches of land which had changed from ruined to lively would appear blue. The areas still laden with toxic air, meanwhile, would look red. Duncan rebooted the display, activating the new program, and the three Masters in the *Wind Raider* waited. Krass grew impatient immediately. She wondered aloud how long it would take. Cringer guessed that it might be hours before they saw any results.

"Can't you power up and Speed Build?" she asked Duncan.

"Not even the Power of Grayskull can force a computer to boot faster."

"We need a backup plan," Adam suggested, "in case this doesn't work."

"No, we don't," Krass answered.

Why was she always challenging him? "Krass! Will you give me a break for one second?"

"Nope," she answered, pointing to the display, "because it looks like we've got a Floranian to track."

On the screen, at the edge of an enormous forest, a thin blue line appeared between the deadly red blotches on the map. The trail spread west from there, suffocating the toxic stench, moving closer to the coast.

Kreannot was on the run.

16.

The *Wind Raider* coasted close to the ground over ruined hills and fields, careful to remain out of view of any nearby villages, until they came to the edge of a thick forest. The trees loomed high overhead, standing nearly as tall as the grandest towers in the city of Eternos. Their trunks were thick and strong, covered with yellow and green moss, and Adam could see that their roots stretched far and wide into the soil. The deep forest beyond was hidden in shadow. Cringer carefully steered the ship through a gap in the wall of trees, and Adam had the strange feeling that the forest itself was alive somehow.

"Where are we going?" Krass asked.

Cringer was already starting to land the ship. "I'm parking the

Wind Raider out of sight," he said. "Now let's hurry. We have a plant to track."

After Cringer slipped his metal claws back on, the trio jumped from the ship to the forest floor and raced ahead. The light on the hills softened as the sun dropped low in the sky. The wall of trees behind them glowed a dull orange, and the sky to the west was changing color by the minute. As they hurried north, climbing bleached hills and crossing barren fields, they stopped repeatedly so Cringer could sniff certain leaves or spots of downtrodden grass. This stalled their progress repeatedly, frustrating Krass. "Do you have to smell everything?"

"I'm building an olfactory library," Cringer replied.

"What does that mean?" Krass asked.

"The more I learn of Kreannot's scent, the easier he will be to follow."

This library never was completed, though. The trio had walked no more than a mile through the fields when the wind rose, and a puff of yellow air curled toward them. Adam and Krass covered their noses, trying not to breathe in the rancid odor, but Cringer reacted too late. His sensitive nose was fried. "I can't smell," he said. "I can't smell a thing."

"A member of the tribe uses all their senses," Krass reminded him with a smile, pointing to her eyes.

Indeed, the path of Kreannot was surprisingly easy to spot. Most of the landscape was brown and lifeless, destroyed by the toxic air, but at the top of the next hill, they spotted a wide swath of lush, green grass cutting through the devastation, bordered by flowers of every color and type. This strange green path wound up and over the hills to the west.

"Where do you think he's going?" Adam wondered.

"I don't know," Krass admitted, "but this would be so much easier if we powered up."

"Patience, Krass," Cringer replied. "We should draw as little attention to ourselves as possible. Not to mention that Kreannot knows you as Tiger Tribe cubs, not warriors. We don't want to scare him off. For now, I think it makes sense to call upon our powers only when we truly need them."

"I really don't want to hike over those hills," Krass said. "I think we need our powers now."

"Totally," Adam said with a laugh.

Cringer growled. "Lazy cubs! I don't know how either of you lasted two days in the tribe. I taught you both to run across the jungle and back before lunchtime, and now you're afraid of a few little hills?"

Adam glanced at Krass.

She smirked.

The two of them hurried off at a sprint, leaving the old tiger with a devastatingly late start behind them. Cringer could outrace them with ease, but the cat kept a steady pace at their heels. Adam could almost feel him smiling as he ran behind them. Krass looked happy, too. Happier than he'd seen her in days, really. Adam slowed his pace slightly. He thought that if he let her win this race, she might relax a little and stop with all the comments about his loyalty to the Tiger Tribe. The instant he let her edge ahead a few strides, however, she turned and glared back at him. "No letting me win, Adam. I want this victory fair and square!"

Smiling, he pumped his arms and quickened his pace.

Soon, he pulled even with her.

The path steepened as it cut up the hill. Both of them were breathing heavily. Even Cringer was panting behind them, and by the time they'd reached the top, all three were completely exhausted. Adam flopped and rolled onto the ground. Krass rested her elbows on her knees, removed her helmet, then stood with her hands behind her head, pacing as she gathered her breath. Neither of them looked down the other side of the hill to the lands beyond. Not at first. Then Cringer uttered a low growl.

The swath of verdant green and brightly colored flowers wound down through the farms and fields to a bustling city surrounding a wide harbor. Dozens of sailing ships of all shapes and sizes were tied to the docks, or else anchored in the still water. The notorious pirate port of Westwind could have been plucked out of another time, deep in Eternia's uncivilized past. And Kreannot's path led straight into the vile, rambunctious heart of the city.

17.

Adam, Cringer, and Krass rushed along the green path into West-wind. Kreannot's trail weaved between scattered houses on the outskirts of the port city, then disappeared when it reached the cobblestone streets of the town. Adam stopped and studied the scene. A horse-drawn cart clattered past. Down a side street, he noticed a small garden crammed between two homes. If anything had been growing there, it wasn't any longer. The toxic wind had struck the city, too, and Adam couldn't see a single plant growing nearby. Not even a weed.

Cringer stopped where the first road met the stones. His sense of smell was finally restored; he leaned down and sniffed the ground. His pace quickened. Krass raced ahead of the tiger. Adam thought she was just in a rush again, but then she stopped and crouched. "Look!" she said.

She was pointing to a recently trampled flower that had grown up between two stones. The crushed purple leaves were still bright. "Granamyr said plants and flowers bloom when a Floranian settles in a grove," she said. "Maybe the same thing happens when Kreannot's moving."

"Interesting theory, Krass," Cringer replied.

"If I'm right," Krass continued, pointing at a few more scattered flowers poking up out of the path, "then we follow those."

"Let's go," Adam said.

Although Adam had the sword at his back, and nothing to fear, he felt better letting the tiger lead the way through the dangerous city. The trio stayed in the middle of the narrow street. Low houses with broken and boarded-up windows lined either side. A woman leaned through the window of a ramshackle house and spat on the ground, and the street grew more crowded the further they walked. No one ran when they saw Cringer, but everyone did move out of the tiger's way. Eventually, the street wound downhill to the sprawling yet crowded harbor. A massive schooner was turning out through the entrance to the harbor, its sails full of wind as it headed for the open sea.

"Whoa," Krass whispered, "I've never been to a pirate port before."

"How do you know for sure that it's a pirate port?" Adam asked.

A skinny, toothless man raced across the street in front of them carrying a salt-encrusted wooden chest. A second man chased him, swinging a curved sword and yelling in a language neither Adam nor Krass had ever heard. The first man tripped on an overturned cobblestone. He slammed to the ground, spilling the contents of the chest. A mix of misshapen coins and jewels spilled onto the street. Instantly, a crowd of men, women, and even a few children appeared out of nowhere, tackling and clawing at each other to grab the treasure.

Krass shrugged. "Ships, treasure, swords," she said. "I'm pretty sure it's a pirate port."

Beside them, Cringer lifted his nose. He'd picked up a scent—Adam and Krass knew better than to interrupt him. They followed him down to the water's edge, where a man with large nostrils and a battered tricorn hat sat on a bench. He was one of the only people in the area who hadn't charged in to grab the spilled treasure. He nearly leaped out of his seat when he saw Cringer, though. Instead of greeting them kindly, he belched. The smell was unexpectedly pleasant—almost floral. Krass pointed to the ground, where several more unlikely flowers grew between the stones.

The wind intensified, nearly blowing the man's tricorn hat off his bald head. "Strong breeze today," Adam noted. He realized the man was still struck by Cringer. "He's friendly," Adam added.

"Unless the situation demands otherwise," Cringer noted.

"He talks, too!" the man replied. His voice was as rough as his battered old hat. "Astounding. Don't worry, friend. I'm no fighter. As for the wind, the breeze always blows strong here, and always to the west. That's why they call it Westwind—"

"Duh," Krass cut in.

"Technically, it should be Eastwind, since the breeze blows out of the east, but hey, pirates make their own rules, you know? Anyway, that reliable wind is what makes this such a great port," the man continued. "Anytime we see trouble coming, we can jump in our ships and be gone in an instant." The man stopped and squinted, nearly closing one of his eyes. "You're not bringing trouble here, are you?"

"No," Adam replied, reassuring him. Or at least he didn't want to, anyway. He just wanted to find Kreannot and go.

"Do you need something to eat?" the pirate asked, sitting up straighter. "I own a little restaurant on the harbor. It's a side business. Pirating isn't always reliable as a source of income. We do a lovely roasted chicken—"

"We're not hungry," Krass insisted.

"We're looking for a friend," Adam added.

Cringer pointed his paw at one of the flowers. "He was here, wasn't he?"

"Ah, you're looking for the legendary Moss Man!" the pirate replied. "Yeah, he was here." He pointed his thumb over his shoulder in the direction of the departing ship. "He was supposed to be on that schooner. Pretty excited about it, too. Weirdest thing I've ever seen. Even odder than a Fuzz Bee."[7]

"What was weird?" Adam asked.

"He's a talking tree," Krass reminded him.

"Right," Adam said. "Good point."

"More of a plant, really," the pirate replied. "And yes, that was odd, but we witness all kinds of oddities on the open sea. I'd been planning a little trip myself, but I'm always interested in a deal, and when I said I'd sell Moss Man my ticket, he got so excited that flowers started popping up all over his chest. Gorgeous flowers, too! I traded him my ticket for a few of the beauties."

Krass charged forward and lowered her helmeted head right up next to the man's face. The gemstone pressed into his forehead

---

7 These rare Eternian creatures, coveted as pets, have the bodies of bees and the heads of elephants. The honey they cultivate is revolting.

hard enough to leave a dent. "What did you do with the flowers, daisy breath?"

The man pushed her away. "I ate them."

"Why in the name of Grayskull did you eat them?" Adam asked.

"They looked tasty," the man said. "I have an unusual appetite."

Adam nudged Krass out of the way. He kneeled before the man. "Any idea where Moss Man went? We really need to find him."

"Sure," he replied. "He hurried off with Eugenia instead of getting on the boat. That was odd, too, come to think of it. He was so excited about the trip."

"Eugenia? Who's that?" Cringer asked.

"A vile woman who owns a vile establishment back that way," the pirate said, pointing up the street. "Her food is horrendous, but everyone goes there anyway. One right, one left, and you'll find it easily."

The three friends thanked the pirate and raced back the way they'd come. After a right turn, and then a left, they stopped suddenly as a huge man was thrown out through the busted wooden door of a pub. An enormous lady in a leather apron chased him out into the street. She pulled a long, rusted sword from a scabbard at her side and lifted it high in the air as the man cowered on the ground below her, holding his forearms in front of his face. "I told you to watch him! Where did he go, you worthless piece of hair from a rat's ear?"

"I don't know!" the man yelled.

"Then get out of my sight!"

The man stumbled on the cobblestones as he escaped. Not one of the three Masters realized they'd been staring. The woman with the sword scowled at them. She was at least a head taller than Adam and three times his size. She was built like a bear, with a huge head, thick arms, and legs that seemed too short for someone of her height. Her hair was greasy and thick and bunched together at the back. Her nose was red and her face was covered with a sheen of sweat.

Adam caught her eyeing the handle of the Sword of Power over his shoulder. She glanced at Krass's helmet, too, and then stared at Cringer. Adam didn't like this woman. Not at all.

After a moment, her expression softened. "Can I help you?"

"Are you Eugenia?" Adam asked. She nodded. "We're looking for a friend of ours."

"Tall fellow? Green?" she replied.

The three friends glanced at each other. Adam didn't actually know exactly what he looked like, but that sounded about right. "You've seen him?" Adam asked.

Again, she eyed his sword. She nodded. "Follow me." The three Masters started after her when she spun around and pointed to Adam. "One kid is enough, and this is a civilized establishment," she added. "No tigers allowed."

Krass grabbed Adam by the forearm. "Are you sure this is a good idea?" she asked.

Adam breathed in deeply as the woman opened the door to the pub. In addition to the rough, rowdy patrons inside, he noticed a long row of trampled flowers growing up from between the floorboards. "No, I'm not sure, Krass," he said, "but I think it's a risk I need to take."

Even as he spoke the words, though, he wasn't sure he believed them.

Adam had the distinct feeling he was walking into a trap.

18.

The restaurant was packed full of boisterous, red-faced men and women, all singing, fighting, and dancing. The more civilized ones among them crowded around rickety tables, playing cards. Food and drinks were spilling and splashing everywhere. A half-filled silver mug crashed into Adam's shoulder, soaking half of his vest. The woman turned back and waved him onward. "Ignore them," she said. "They're all harmless."

"Sure," Adam muttered. "Totally harmless."

At the far end of the crowded room, the giant hostess opened a heavy wooden door with a huge iron clasp for a handle, then led him down a hallway and through another door into a darkened room. "Wait in here," she said, pushing Adam inside. "There are some very comfortable chairs in the middle of the room. Have a seat and relax. I'll be back with your friend in a minute."

When the heavy door slammed shut, the space turned as dark as a Snake Mountain crypt. Adam couldn't even see the walls or the ceiling. Yet it felt like a large room—as cavernous as one of the great halls of Castle Grayskull. The only sounds were the muffled voices and roars from the bar. Adam decided he'd feel much, much better about the whole situation if he turned into He-Man, but he didn't want to draw any unnecessary attention.

Carefully, he crept forward, holding his hands out in front of him.

Where were those chairs she was talking about?

Suddenly he heard a loud clang, the sound of chains moving.

Something gigantic and heavy dropped down around him.

The floor shook from the force.

Instinctively, Adam reached for the sword, but powerful hands grabbed him by the back of his vest and slammed him against heavy iron bars.

And the sword . . . the sword was gone.

Stunned, Adam turned and reached out. Everywhere he turned, he bumped up against iron bars.

His host began laughing. "Well, that was easier than I thought!"

"What are you doing?" Adam asked. "Give me back my sword!"

The woman struck a match and lit a huge torch. The light revealed that his situation was as bad as he'd imagined. Adam hadn't just lost the Sword of Power. He was trapped inside a massive cage. He-Man could have bent the bars aside. Ram Ma'am might have been able to crash her way in. And Battle Cat's claws would have sliced straight through the metal. But his friends weren't there to help him. Adam was powerless.

He watched the woman as she circled the room. Her face was even more monstrous in the flickering light from the torch. She crossed to the far wall and swung open a set of tall wooden shutters. Sunlight streamed inside, revealing glass display cases of varying sizes. Inside were the bony remains of birds, fish, and all other kinds of creatures, including what looked like a young dragon. Apparently, his hostess had an unsettling fondness for skeletons.

"Why, in the name of Randor, would I give you back your sword?" she asked. "If I'm guessing correctly, this is that magical sword I've heard rumors about. How a little runt like you ended up with it is beyond me, but I imagine this lovely weapon will fetch quite a reward from that handsome new tyrant."

Now she was planning to give it to Skeletor? Seriously?

This was beyond bad. This was a multidimensional disaster.

Plus, she thought Skeletor was handsome.

That was more frightening than anything else.

"I could pay you instead," Adam suggested.

She turned the sword upside down, resting the tip on the floor and her hands on the bottom of the handle. "Pay me what?" she asked.

Adam was surprised how much it bothered him to see someone else holding the Sword of Power. On one level, he was annoyed. The weapon belonged to him, and no one else. Not Skeletor, and certainly not this woman. But another part of him was just plain devastated. He'd been entrusted with the weapon by Castle

Grayskull itself. Now some ruffian restaurateur was going to give it back to Skeletor? So much for defending the planet.

Adam couldn't even defend himself.

As for paying the woman, well, that was tricky. Technically, Adam was the prince of Eternos, but he didn't actually have any money himself. Plus, his dad wasn't even on the throne anymore. "I'm going to be honest with you," he said. "I don't have any money. But I really, really need that sword, and I need to find Moss Man. Was he here?"

"Yes, he was here. Right inside that very cage, in fact. He'd been planning to sail away when I promised him I could arrange a much better trip, to far more interesting lands, so he agreed to follow me. I always know an adventurer when I spot one. I'm pretty good at picking out the gullible folks, too. I was hoping to add him to my collection, and he was very disappointed when he found out I was lying about the promised trip. He slipped through my trap, the wily weed." She ran the sword along the bars; the clang of metal and Kirbinite against iron was surprisingly dull. Desperately, Adam reached out to grab the blade, but she yanked it back. Then her eyes brightened. "I just had a fantastic idea! I believe we can make an arrangement that satisfies us both."

"What do you mean?" Adam asked.

"My collection here includes specimens of some of the rarest species on Eternia. That one there, for example"—she pointed at an odd, winged skeleton—"is the remains of a wolfbat from the Banshee Jungle. Very few of those in existence! But a Floranian? That would be the crown jewel. So . . ."

She leaned forward, smiling.

Adam felt an unsettling chill. "Yes?"

"If I release you, and you capture the Floranian for me"—her voice changed, adopting an almost friendly tone—"I'll give you back your sword."

Adam gripped the iron bars. He gritted his teeth. "No," he snapped. "No creature deserves to be trapped in one of your cages."

"No deal then?"

"No deal," Adam replied.

Eugenia shrugged her huge shoulders, then reached into one of her pockets, removed a handheld communicator, and held it up to her ear. "Oh well, then I suppose I'll call the palace. Does this Skeletor fellow like swords? I heard he's more of a staff and scepter type. He'll love this one, though. It's so unique."

Adam thought of his friends outside waiting for him. They'd come looking for him soon. "If you don't give me back that sword," Adam warned her, "my two friends are going to take it from you."

"The girl and that overgrown kitten?" Eugenia replied. "I think my men and I will manage just fine against them. Now I've wasted far too much time with you already, young man. Thank you for the sword. If you behave, I'll release you in the morning."

Adam leaned back against the bars of the cage and slid down to the floor. He was trying not to abandon hope when he heard the slow, careful creak of a window opening. Squinting, he bolted upright and spotted what looked like a vine snaking into the room. The vine was as thick as one of his arms and covered with leaves and patches of bright moss. It curved left and right as it crossed the floor, as if searching for something. When the vine reached the iron bars of his cage, it curled and snaked up around them. Then it seemed to thicken and strengthen before tilting the cage onto its side, opening a gap between the base and the floor.

Adam wasted no time; he rolled out of his iron prison, then watched as the vine retracted toward the open window. He glanced back at the door. Eugenia had gone that way with the Sword of Power. And he desperately needed it back. But he suspected that the strange vine wasn't just some magical root. He had a feeling he'd finally found Kreannot, and he wasn't about to let him get away.

19.

One of the first skills you mastered in the Tiger Tribe was the art of climbing. Trees, rocks, mountainsides—the cubs learned to scale them all. Now Adam put his skills to work, scurrying up the wall and out the window. He dropped into a narrow, muddy alley. His boots splashed into a puddle. He called out to Cringer and Krass, hoping they'd hear him, then followed the retreating vine away from the street, into the darkness between the buildings. A door swung open unexpectedly, and a man in a stained apron tossed a huge pot full of vegetable scraps into the alley. Adam leaped over the stalks and rinds.

Ahead, the alley forked in two directions. The path to the left turned sharply, but the one to the right curved off, and he spotted the last tendrils of the vine moving that way. He charged forward.

The path soon came to a dead end. The buildings all around him were tall enough to block out the setting sun. They almost seemed to lean toward one another. The vine had stopped retreating, too, and Adam watched as it recoiled around what looked like the base of a small green tree. A second trunk stood beside it, and Adam decided they didn't look like trees so much as the very, very thick stalks of two plants.

No, he realized, those were legs.

Slowly, carefully, Adam raised his head.

But Kreannot still wasn't ready to be seen.

The walls around Adam were suddenly bursting with plant life. Flowers, leaves, and vines rushed through a season's worth of growth in an instant. A screen of greenery blocked Adam's view of the Floranian. He backed away. "I'm not here to hurt you!" Adam called to him. He lowered his voice, trying to sound friendly. "We need your help."

"I hardly think you could hurt me, and I just helped you out of that cage."

"I know. Thank you! I met you once before—"

"Where?"

"In the jungle," Adam answered. "Near the territory of the Tiger Tribe. You were chasing away a Pelleezean named Odiphus."

Two eyes appeared briefly in the screen of greenery, then disappeared. "No. Impossible. The kid I met there was . . . younger."

"That was two years ago. I've grown. My name is Adam, remember?"

The Floranian laughed. The sound was strange; a mix of snapping twigs and rustling leaves. "Oh, right. I forget how quickly you humans age. How can I help you, Adam?"

"Maybe you could drop the screen first?"

Huge hands pulled aside the greenery, and Adam had his first real look at the legendary Moss Man. He was shaped like a person, but had thick green stalks instead of legs, with vines winding tightly around them. His enormous, muscular chest looked like . . . well, Adam decided, it actually reminded him of moss. Which kind of made sense. And he was powerfully built, with thick, vine-encased arms, a square jaw, and massive green hands. His hair looked like overgrown, matted-down grass, and a thick, mossy unibrow stretched across his face above his greenish-yellow eyes. The Floranian smiled awkwardly, and Adam wasn't entirely surprised to see that his teeth were green, too. "I'm not used to being looked at," Kreannot said, shrinking back into the corner. "I don't like it."

A flower blooming on his shoulder wilted.

"Are you okay?" Adam asked. He pointed to the flower. "Does that mean you're hurt?"

"Oh, that?" Kreannot replied, glancing at the flower. "That happens sometimes when I'm unhappy."

"I didn't mean to make you unhappy . . ."

"It's not you," Kreannot said. "It's this city. And that woman. What a horrible place! I was planning to hide out and escape tonight, in the dark, when I heard her take you captive."

"Why did you help me?"

"I like helping other creatures," Kreannot replied. "Plus, you refused to make that deal with her. I felt I owed you after that."

Adam eyed the wilting flower again. "If you're unhappy here, what makes you happy?"

"Traveling! Seeing the world! Not staying rooted in one spot like the rest of my kind." Kreannot crossed his viny arms over his mossy chest. "Now, you said you need my help. What is it that you need?"

"Your mossflowers."

Surprised, the Floranian leaned back his head. "My flowers?"

"Long story, but there's a toxic gas spreading all over the planet. It's Pelleezean. I'm pretty sure it's the creation of our old friend Odiphus, the one who threatened you in the jungle."

"Yesterday, right?"

"No, I told you. That was two years ago."

"Ah, right. Our sense of time is different," Kreannot replied. "But I do remember that misguided Pelleezean. Normally, their kind are wonderful. They have tremendous appetites. They'll eat almost anything. And they are fantastic diggers, as you learned. Some of them are quite wealthy thanks to their work in construction, digging foundations and such, but their species has been in a sad state for centuries, on account of their smell. No one ever lets them settle anywhere. Personally, I love to move, but I can see how it would be heartbreaking if you wanted to build a home and you were always being chased away."

Adam nodded along with Kreannot. He admired the Floranian's heart. And he felt for the Pelleezeans, too. But the toxic odor problem was a little more pressing. "Back in the jungle, your mossflowers counteracted that Pelleezean perfume. My friends Krass and Cringer—"

"The tiger, right? Great kid."

"Actually, he's super old," Adam said. Briefly, Adam marveled at the creature's twisted sense of time. Cringer had last seen the Floranian decades before. Yet to Kreannot, it probably felt like a few weeks. Adam continued. "Anyway, we think we'll be able to use your mossflowers to fight the toxic gas. We could save fields, woods, jungles, and farms all over Eternia. As long as this gas spreads, every plant on the planet is in danger, but we can stop that and help them all. So I guess what I'm asking is . . . will you help us?"

The creature's unibrow rose. "Yes."

"You will?"

"Of course I will! Just because I don't interact with humans doesn't mean I don't care about your kind." Kreannot stared back down the alley, then up into the darkening sky. "The thought of so much of my plant family perishing is terrifying, too. Yet I won't be able to bloom here in this city any longer. The only reason I was able to earlier is that I was so thrilled by the prospect of a sailing adventure!" He shivered slightly. "I never should've listened to that lady."

Adam thought immediately of the forest. "Beyond the hills there are trees—"

"Yes! I have relatives in the area. There's a very special grove in the forest, due east from here. Why don't you follow me?"

Relatives? What was Kreannot talking about? Plus, Adam couldn't go with him yet anyway. First, he had to retrieve the Sword of Power. "I'll meet you there," he said. "How do I find this grove?"

"A waterfall pours out from between two great stones and into a deep, clear pool. Follow the sound of the water. I'll wait for you."

At that, Kreannot climbed up and over the rooftops before Adam could say goodbye. Although Adam watched him scurry away, neither the plant nor the young hero noticed the odd shimmer in the air above the roof, where the invisible, cloaked Tri-Klops drone had been silently hovering, recording their every word.

20.

Adam raced out of the alleyway to the street in front of the pub, where his two friends waited impatiently. Krass spotted him first. "What happened?" she asked. "Did you find him?"

"I found him," Adam answered. "He agreed to help us. We're going to meet him in the forest. Apparently, he has family nearby?"

"Interesting," Cringer remarked.

"Um, Adam, where's the sword?" Krass asked.

"Eugenia grabbed it," he answered, "and before we go anywhere, I need to get it back."

Cringer growled. "Leave this one to me, cubs."

Adam smiled, and Krass patted the tiger's back. "No offense, but you're kind of old," she said. "Plus, they did say no tigers are allowed inside."

The tiger leaped forward and pounced on the wooden door, knocking it flat to the floor inside. The crowded pub turned silent. The stench of sweat and mold was almost as powerful as the toxic perfume. Cringer reared back on his hind paws, let out a huge, window-rattling growl, and sprang into the chaos.

Krass crouched, staggered her feet, leaned forward, and lowered her right shoulder, as if she were ready to power up.

Adam grabbed her at the elbow. "Wait," he said.

"We need to help him!" Krass shouted.

"We don't want to make any more of a scene," Adam replied, "and you know how proud he is—he wants to show that he still has some fight in him, even without the Power of Grayskull. We have to give him a chance."

"One minute," Krass snapped. "That's all."

But they didn't need to wait that long.

Inside the bar, they heard someone yell, and then one of the half-broken front windows shattered completely as Cringer flew backward out onto the street.

"See!" Krass said. "We should have helped!"

The tiger rolled over onto his side. Adam feared he was seriously hurt. Then he noticed his old friend clutching something wrapped in thick canvas. Smiling, the tiger tossed the bundle onto the cobblestones. The canvas unfurled, revealing the handle, hilt, and blade of a very familiar sword. Adam didn't need to wait for Krass or Cringer to urge him to grab the weapon; he dashed to the tiger's side and wrapped his fingers around the handle.

The chaos inside the pub only increased, and he heard Eugenia roar, "Get outside and fetch me that sword!"

Cringer struggled to his paws. "I believe it's time we powered up, cubs."

Before the crowds poured out and spotted his face, Adam wrapped both hands around the Sword of Power, held it in front of him, and declared, "BY THE POWER OF GRAYSKULL!" Lightning crackled in the sky. Bright yellow bolts of mystical energy shot down and into the sword. The blade grew, doubling and then tripling in size. Adam felt himself expanding from the inside out. He'd never felt better, or stronger, in his life, as he raised the sword high and intoned, "I HAVE THE POWER!"

Streaks and sparks shot out of the gemstone on Krass's helmet. Armored, rocket-powered boots covered her legs. Her helmet transformed into the Grayskull-infused Helm of Destruction and energy flowed all around her.

Meanwhile, Cringer grew to three times his normal size. His metal claws radiated yellow. His head and back were encased in impenetrable armor, and he roared so loud that the very buildings around them shook.

When the energy settled and the sky cleared, the three heroes stood beside each other on the street. The ruffians streamed out of the pub. Two of the men quickly dashed back inside, having no interest in fighting the warriors. But at least two dozen thugs poured out, surrounding the friends.

Eugenia sneered at Battle Cat. "You look different, kitty. I see you brought friends, too."

"Have you changed your mind?" Battle Cat asked. "We'd be happy to leave here in peace."

"No one's leaving without a fight," she snapped. "I don't care who've you got on your side."

"Yeah, well, that's a mistake," Rammy replied. "Hey, He-Man?"

"Yes, Rammy?"

"Leave her to me. You two sweep up the rest of this garbage."

"With pleasure," Battle Cat growled.

The fight that ensued wasn't exactly a fair one. The Masters were outnumbered by eight to one, and the thugs were armed with swords, knives, clubs, and any weapon they could find. One giant pub patron snapped off the leg of a table and swung it at Battle Cat, but the tiger swiped away the attempted blow. Then he pounced on the man's chest, nearly knocking him out, and crushed the improvised weapon in his jaws. He-Man hardly even used his sword. He swung it once, to knock down a knife thrown at his chest, but otherwise his hands were powerful enough. He was still getting used to his incredible strength, though, and he accidentally punched his first attacker straight through a wall. Thankfully, the man was huge, so the blow didn't hurt him permanently. But it was enough to convince the brute that he wasn't going to win a fight against He-Man. Dazed, he staggered off through a side alley.

Worried about hurting anyone too badly, He-Man tried to imagine he was merely swatting flies, not punching pirates. Even when he'd barely tap his attackers, though, they'd drop as if they'd been struck by sledgehammers. And when they punched him back, he didn't even feel it. One woman leaped off a cart and cracked a wooden chair over his back and it actually tickled.

The hostess was sitting upright against the side of her pub, dazed and defeated, as Rammy bounced between the buildings like an electrified pinball. In less than a minute, all of their attackers were either rolling on the ground, sitting against walls, or hurrying away into the alleys.

The owner didn't even have the strength to sneer. "Fine," Eugenia said. "You win."

21.

The three Masters raced out through the town to the base of the hills, relieved that Skeletor and his minions hadn't tracked them down in time. Rammy stopped and closed one eye, staring at the path as if she were estimating something. Then she turned to He-Man. "Roll me."

"What?" Battle Cat asked.

"I'm talking to Mr. Muscles here," she replied, pointing to He-Man. "Roll me up that hill as hard as you can."

"Need I remind you, Ram Ma'am, that you can catapult yourself?" Battle Cat asked.

Rammy shrugged. "I know," she said, "but this'll be fun!"

He-Man eyed the slope. Then he hoisted his friend like a bowling ball, took several steps back, and hurled her along the path with his unlimited might. Rammy rocketed up the side of the hill. He-Man couldn't even see his friend anymore—she transformed into a bright, colorful sphere. With sparks shooting out in every direction, she sped straight up over the side, arcing through the air.

"Jump on my back," Battle Cat yelled. "We've got some catching up to do!"

As He-Man held on, the huge tiger raced up the side of the hill in several giant leaps. He couldn't fly like Sorceress, or accelerate like Rammy, but Battle Cat could run. He-Man leaned forward, holding onto the armored saddle. Battle Cat's claws dug into the grass and dirt. The powerful muscles in his legs launched them high into the air. Rammy was the one who'd been looking forward to having some fun, but He-Man got the distinct sense that his old tiger friend was enjoying himself, too.

Together, Battle Cat and He-Man cleared three hills in a flash, hurried across the half-dead field, then stopped at the edge of the dark forest.

Rammy was waiting for them. She smacked the side of the Helm of Destruction. Then she shook her head, dizzy. "That *was* fun," she declared. "But next time I think I'll launch myself."

"Hey!"

A familiar voice was calling out to them—the friends turned to see an armored figure racing out of the woods to the south. Duncan had transformed into Man-at-Arms, and he covered the distance between them quickly. Then he swung his Power Mace up over his shoulder, flipped open his visor, and smiled.

"How did you find us?" He-Man asked.

"Tracked the *Wind Raider*," Man-at-Arms replied with a shrug. "Then I jumped on a Sky Sled to get here. Quick trip. Those things are fast! But that forest is spooky." He shivered. "I feel much better all powered up."

With no small degree of sarcasm, Battle Cat added, "I'm delighted that you had an enjoyable journey, but you're supposed to be protecting Castle Grayskull."

"Hey, don't worry!" Man-at-Arms replied, holding up his armored hands. "The magical castle in the clouds is just fine. I've got robot sentries flying all around Avion."

"What are you even doing here?" Rammy asked.

Battle Cat growled. "You're not checking on the *Wind Raider*, are you?"

Guilty, Man-at-Arms shrugged. "She's my baby! I wanted to make sure you didn't ruin her. Plus, I finished that assignment you gave me. Built a sweet little molecular analyzer and aerosolized compound replicator for when you find Kreannot. It's back on the Sky Sled."

Rammy glanced at He-Man, who turned to Battle Cat. He-Man realized he and his two friends were equally confused. None of them understood what in Eternia Man-at-Arms was talking about.

"This is the part where you explain, Dinky," Rammy said. "In normal language."

"Oh, right," Man-at-Arms replied. He stared down at the ground for a second. Then he lifted a finger in the air, opened his mouth as if he was going to speak, and stopped again. This happened a few more times, in the span of only a few seconds, before he finally explained. "So, basically, you guys get a few of these mossflowers, we pop them in my machine, and then the machine copies the smell, turns it into digital information, sends that to all the other artificial noses we've got flying around Eternia, and they puff it out."

He-Man thought about this for a moment. "Almost like they're . . . sneezing?" he asked.

Man-at-Arms scrunched his eyes. "Sort of? Maybe. Yes . . . sure! That works. We're going to trigger one giant artificial sneeze in the planet's atmosphere and basically kill off the toxic odor."

"That's brilliant," Battle Cat said.

The young inventor tapped the side of his head. "Didn't even need the Power of Grayskull to come up with that one," he added.

He-Man climbed off Battle Cat's back. "Great work," the champion said, slapping his friend on the back in gratitude. He still hadn't quite learned how to control his strength, though, so he accidentally knocked him to the ground. "Sorry!"

Man-at-Arms jumped up and brushed some grass off one of his armored shoulders. Then He-Man noticed Battle Cat staring back in the direction of the town. "What's wrong?"

"Skeletor should be here by now," Battle Cat replied. "Yet we haven't seen any sign of him."

He-Man shrugged his huge shoulders. "We should consider that good luck. Let's find Kreannot, get the mossflowers, and get out of here before Bonehead does find us."

The woods were eerily quiet. He-Man led the way, listening for the waterfall. The trees were spaced far apart. Each one was so large that not even He-Man would have been able to wrap his arms around their trunks. Some stood taller than Randor's palace, and they were covered with thick moss. The ground was scattered with ferns as tall as Ram Ma'am and rocks the size of Battle Cat's head. There was no clear path through the forest, so He-Man cut a trail with some easy swings of the Sword of Power.

He-Man was beginning to wonder if they'd gone the wrong way when they reached the rim of a wide, circular grove. The ground sloped down from the rim and flattened out. To his right, water rushed between two enormous, jagged boulders, pouring into a deep, clear pool surrounded by still more stones. All around the grove loomed the largest trees any of them had ever seen. The place was stunningly beautiful.

Even Ram Ma'am felt the serenity of the spot. "It's so . . . peaceful," she murmured.

This had to be the spot, He-Man decided. But Kreannot said he had family in the area, and while a few of the trees were blooming with strange and beautiful flowers, nothing here was moving like a Floranian. The trees and plants were all thoroughly rooted to the ground. Maybe this was a good sign, though, He-Man thought. Granamyr had mentioned something about how most Floranians bloomed when they were happily rooted in their chosen spot. Was this one of those groves? Were they surrounded by Kreannot's kind?

With the Sword of Power at his side, He-Man inched forward.

The sun hadn't set long before, but the branches of the huge trees entwined overhead, blocking what little light remained.

The grove was peaceful, as Rammy said, but it was almost too quiet. No birds sang. No beetles buzzed. The only sounds were the careful footsteps of the Masters and the rush of the waterfall.

As He-Man crept down the slope, he noticed a faint green light glowing from behind one of the trees in the center of the grove. He felt a sudden pit in his stomach. Not fear, exactly, but a sensation that something had gone horribly wrong, and that their situation was turning quickly in a darker direction. On the far side of the tree, Kreannot was anchored in place by glowing green chains.

Then a very familiar, very chilling laugh resounded through the grove.

Skeletor had found them at last.

22.

The Dark Master of Havoc stepped out of the darkness, wielding his staff. Beneath his purple hood, his eyes glowed red inside the cavities of his skull. He clenched his bony left hand into a fist and pointed the ram's head atop his staff at Kreannot. The staff glowed green with the primordial energy of Havoc, the mystical fuel that powered him.

Next, the snarling, growling Beast Man leaped down from a tree, landing on the ground on all fours and cracking his deadly whip, the Lash of Beasts, with a resonant and terrifying snap. His red eyes shone devilishly. Trap Jaw stomped out of the shadows after him, wielding what looked like a huge cannon as his right arm. His head was cocked back confidently.

"Release our friend!" He-Man shouted.

Skeletor sidestepped closer to Kreannot, then leaned toward him, as if he were considering meeting He-Man's request. The Havoc staff glowed. A cloud of the evil green energy swirled near the Floranian. Finally, Skeletor stood up and shrugged. "No, I don't think so," Skeletor replied. "I plan to trap him here until he has become so rooted to this soil that he can never leave again."

"You don't understand, Skeletor," Battle Cat interrupted.

"Quiet, kitty!" growled Beast Man, snapping his whip again.

"No one calls me—"

He-Man stepped in front of his friend, hoping Skeletor might listen. "What Battle Cat was trying to say," He-Man interrupted, "is that Kreannot can help save the people of Eternos."

Skeletor laughed. "Save people? Why would I want to save people?"

"You're supposed to be their king now," Rammy said.

"You're supposed to look out for them," Man-at-Arms added.

"I know how to rule!" Skeletor shouted. "I understand power far better than any of you. I also know that this disaster is my brother's fault."

The most savage of the Dark Masters cracked his whip. "Beast Man tracked the scent from the site of the big train crash. Beast Man was the one who figured out that Randor had hidden the toxic perfume."

"Why is Beast Man talking about himself in the third person?" He-Man asked.

"That's his *thing*," Skeletor snapped. "And I am so proud of you, Beastie-my-Bestie. Back to this whole helping people bit, though—why would I reverse Randy's errors?"

"Because innocent people could starve!" He-Man noted.

"Yes, and when they starve, I'll make sure they all know that it's the fault of that fool Randor."

This was more than He-Man could tolerate. King Randor wasn't perfect. When Adam had disappeared as a kid, and Eldress had left him in the jungle of the Tiger Tribe, the king had given up searching for him a little too easily. The tribe wasn't *that* far from Eternos. Plus, as Teela had said, his father cared more about keeping the peace with Avion than he did about the people living in the Lower Wards beneath his palace. His father was flawed. But Randor was still his dad, and He-Man wasn't going to let Skeletor insult him like that.

He lifted the Sword of Power over his head and charged.

Skeletor swung his Havoc staff toward the champion.

A blast of the primordial green energy shot out of the ram's head.

Holding the Sword of Power out in front of him, He-Man pushed forward through the raging Havoc. Each step required all of his strength. He felt like he was pushing the *Eternia 2000* up a mountainside. Yet he was moving.

Slowly, but steadily, he was inching closer to the hooded villain.

Suddenly, the Havoc recoiled.

Skeletor turned his staff, flipped it in the air, grabbed the base with both hands, and swung it down toward He-Man's head with enough power to slam a normal human into the depths of the planet.

Yet the staff never struck the champion. He-Man dropped to one knee and raised the Sword of Power, stopping the blow.

The two rivals stood locked in this position, each pushing back with all of his formidable strength. Then, at the same time, each of them made a final, desperate push—and the pair were blasted back to opposite sides of the clearing.

Twin flashes of green Havoc and golden Grayskull energy exploded through the grove.

He-Man somersaulted backward. He shook his head. The blow had stung, but he wasn't injured. He sprang to his feet. "How did you beat us here, Skeletor?"

The tyrant lifted his clawlike left hand and twirled it in the air. "We've been tracking you fools, and one of my new toys, Tri-Klops, eavesdropped on your conversation in the alley, He-Man. You should take better note of your surroundings next time, nephew. You never know who's listening."

"Umm, Skeletor?" Man-at-Arms interrupted. He was holding up the Power Mace as if he were raising his hand. "Why do you even want Moss Man? I mean, I sort of get the whole blaming-it-on-your-brother thing, but don't you think you'd be better off helping us, and saving people?"

"And other creatures," Battle Cat noted.

"That would be way more popular," Rammy added.

The villain stared at Ram Ma'am. "Hello again, dear. Have you been thinking about that question I asked you?" Rammy froze. Skeletor laughed and turned back to He-Man. "I'm sorry. Just a quick little sidebar with your friend, Wee-Man. As for this hapless tree creature, I think you misunderstand. I don't want Moss Man. I want you to tell me how to find Grayskull, you foolish child, so that I can destroy it!"

The cannon at the end of Trap Jaw's arm spun as he added, "We're going to blast that pile of rocks into oblivion."

"Yeah," Beast Man snarled, "what they said."

Skeletor sighed with frustration, and He-Man could see his red eyes rolling under his hood. "Beastie-my-Bestie? Please be quiet. You're embarrassing us. Now, He-Man, tell me where to find the castle and I'll let this sentient weed go free. If you refuse, however, I'll see to it that Moss Man never blooms again. The toxic air will kill every living plant. Your father will get all the blame and my grip on this planet will only be stronger."

"But . . . why?" Man-at-Arms asked.

"Because I don't want to be popular," Skeletor replied. "I want to be powerful."

"You'll never find Grayskull again," He-Man insisted.

Battle Cat roared in agreement.

The hooded tyrant slammed his staff against the forest floor. "I'll pretend you didn't say that, nephew," Skeletor snapped. "Tell me what I want to know or Eternia becomes a lifeless desert. *Where is Grayskull?*"

"Up your bony nose!" Rammy yelled.

The hot-tempered hero instantly fired up the rockets in her helmet and armor and shot herself across the grove at the Dark Master of Havoc. Skeletor leaped out of the way at the last instant, and the scene devolved into chaos. Trap Jaw activated his cannon arm. The muzzle of the weapon spun faster and faster until it was sparkling with energy. He aimed for Rammy first, but she dodged the blast, and the laser exploded at the base of a huge tree.

The energy was still pulsing through his weapon, so Trap Jaw fired again and again at Rammy. She darted from tree to tree at first. Then she stopped changing directions. She circled the clearing, building speed, moving faster and faster—a blur of light and energy. The king's old weapons master couldn't hope to hit her now, so he swung his cannon toward his former assistant.

Instinctively, Man-at-Arms lifted his Power Mace, generating a force-field shield. The blasts from Trap Jaw's cannon ricocheted off the orange shield and up through the canopy. Yet Man-at-Arms had a few surprise weapons of his own—back at the Castle, he'd modified two of the extra air sensors, turning them into tiny laser drones. As Trap Jaw attacked, he lobbed one into the air, then the other.

As Battle Cat leaped toward Beast Man, the Dark Master snapped his savage, spinelike Lash of Beasts, stunning the tiger. Then Beast Man dug his sharp claws into the ground and jumped at Battle Cat. The pair met in a colossal midair crash.

The scene had devolved into a Grayskull- and Havoc-powered rumble.

He-Man wanted to help his friends, but he had to trust they could fend for themselves. As he watched Rammy speeding around the grove, though, he wondered if this was true. Did she even have a plan?

Or was she totally out of control?

Across the way, Skeletor was twirling his Havoc staff.

The spherical blur of energy was heading straight for him.

Rammy, apparently, was planning to smash He-Man's uncle.

Unfortunately, Skeletor was ready, and blasted her with a stream of Havoc before she could get too close.

The stunned Master rolled straight between Trap Jaw and Man-at-Arms.

Trap Jaw was moving closer and closer to his old apprentice, firing blast after blast at the shield. "You should be working at my side, not helping these fools," Trap Jaw yelled.

"At your side?" Man-at-Arms replied. "You took credit for everything I built!"

"I taught you everything you know."

"That is so not true." Man-at-Arms replied. "You saw me build a self-defense robot as a six-year-old kid."

Trap Jaw nodded, stopping his onslaught for a moment. "That was impressive."

"You did teach me a little about drones, though," Man-at-Arms admitted.

With a smile, he motioned at the flying lasers hovering over Trap Jaw.

Yet the Dark Master showed no fear. Instead, he opened his mouth, activating the spinning, terrifying Maw of Weaponry, and sucked in the laser drones one by one. Quickly, the cannon at the end of his arm changed shape, transforming into a laser chainsaw. Smiling, Trap Jaw swung it at a nearby tree, slicing the trunk in half. "Thanks for that, little guy," Trap Jaw growled. "I love the taste of lasers."

Man-at-Arms didn't wait to see if the chainsaw could cut through his shield, too. While Trap Jaw stood gloating over his instant invention, Man-at-Arms dropped the force field and swung his Power Mace, striking his old boss right in his muscular stomach. The blow blasted the villain across the clearing.

Immediately, Man-at-Arms looked to his friends to see who needed his help. He-Man and Skeletor were locked in a one-on-one battle. Rammy was accelerating around the space, and Battle Cat was pinning Beast Man up against the trunk of a tree. His huge paws pressed into the snarling villain, and it looked like he'd gotten the best of Skeletor's Dark Master.

Then Beast Man smiled one of the ugliest smiles in all of Eternia. His lips were scarred, puffy, and purple. His teeth were yellow and green. His red beard was a scraggly, knotted mess, and his breath smelled like a rotting gorgon carcass.

But his timing was perfect.

Beast Man pushed back against Battle Cat just as Rammy sped past, and she accidentally crashed into the fearsome tiger.

The pair rolled out of the clearing, leaving a long dirt track in their wake.

Worried for his friends, He-Man called out to see if they were hurt.

He only took his attention off Skeletor for an instant, but that was enough. The bony villain pulled back on his Havoc staff, then swung it through a wide, powerful arc. With his legs braced and both hands clutching the weapon, he slammed it hard into He-Man's ribs.

The power of the blow sent He-Man flying off the ground and against the trunk of an enormous tree. Dazed, he fell to the base of the tree, sliding down the thick, moss-covered roots. Finally, he rolled to a stop on his back. His ribs ached. Yet he had a strange feeling that he wasn't the only one who'd been hurt by the strike. He even thought he'd heard an odd grunt. He-Man leaned his head back and looked up. The thick, towering, moss-lined tree seemed to lean over him as if it were alive. The petals of several unusual flowers drifted down. He-Man blinked. Was he seeing things? Or had he woken up one of Kreannot's relatives?

His whole body was in pain. He felt like he'd been hit by the *Wind Raider*. He knew that any lesser human might not have survived that strike from Skeletor. But He-Man was not a normal human. He was infused with the Power of Grayskull, and it would take more than one powerful blow to defeat him.

Gathering his strength, he rolled onto his hands and knees. He placed one of his huge fists into the dirt and gritted his teeth. Before he could climb to his feet, however, Skeletor blasted him again. Still groggy, He-Man didn't notice the glowing ram's head at the top of Skeletor's staff until it was right in front of his eyes, and this second blow was even more painful and powerful than the first. The staff slammed him in the chin, and the might of Skeletor lifted the hero straight off the ground and against the tree. Stunned, He-Man felt his back and head smack against the trunk with one great thud.

He tried to gather his breath, but Skeletor wasted no time. Green light flashed from his Havoc staff and wrapped around the hero, holding him in place.

He-Man struggled against what felt like unbreakable chains.

Every square inch of him was trapped by Havoc.

He couldn't even move a finger, let alone a fist.

Laughing, the villain lifted him slowly off the ground until He-Man's feet were at the level of Skeletor's chest. The hero couldn't run or jump, and although he still gripped the sword, his arms were pinned against his sides. He-Man felt powerless, and he could see that his friends were no better off. Beast Man had his deadly whip poised and ready to strike. Somehow, Trap Jaw had snagged the Power Mace from Man-at-Arms. Meanwhile, poor Kreannot remained immobilized.

Skeletor stood before He-Man. The villain's hood masked most of his head and face, enshrouding it in darkness and shadow. His eyes glowed an evil red. His powerful Havoc staff radiated green, and he was flashing a ghastly and satisfied smile. "Now, little prince," the villain began, "you are going to tell me where you're hiding Castle Grayskull, or your friends will not leave this forest alive, that overgrown vine you're trying to protect will die, and the people of Eternia will starve."

23.

Bright green lights flashed through the canopy overhead as a dozen mind-controlled Red Legion soldiers sped down into the grove on their Sky Sleds. The Havoc-brained guards parked their hover-crafts and marched into place, lining the borders of the grove, waiting for orders from their master. Rammy and Man-at-Arms huddled back-to-back with Battle Cat. Not one of them dared to move, and Kreannot seemed to be weakening by the second. Strangled by Skeletor's Havoc-fueled chains, his body was thinning. His limbs were turning spindly and weak. He-Man's friends needed him now more than ever. Focusing his strength, he tightened his grip on the Sword of Power.

"Easy now, little prince," Skeletor replied.

"Stop calling me that," He-Man growled.

"Oooohhh, is the most powerful man in the universe getting angry?" Skeletor fake-shivered. "I'm so, so very scared."

"If you're so tough," Battle Cat growled, "why don't you release him and fight him fair, without magic?"

"Because I'm not a fool, you overgrown kitty," Skeletor snapped. "Now, my little prince—oh, I'm sorry, my nephew—if you so much as raise that sword, Trap Jaw and Beast Man will finish your helpless friends, and I'll turn your beloved Moss Man to ashes." The glowing Havoc tightened around He-Man. "So I'll ask you again, one more time," Skeletor said, his voice terrifying. "WHERE IS GRAYSKULL?"

Although he had the body of a giant warrior, He-Man was still Adam on the inside. And Adam wouldn't sacrifice his friends for anything. Not even Castle Grayskull. He had to tell Skeletor. Then he just had to trust and hope they could still find a way to stop him from destroying the castle. They were the Masters of the Universe. Together, they could do anything.

The Dark Master of Havoc leaned in closer. Skeletor's breath was cold against his face, and He-Man was getting ready to tell the tyrant what he so desperately wanted to know. Then something strange happened.

He-Man felt the tree behind him moving ever so slightly. Instantly, he thought back to Granamyr's words, and what Kreannot himself had said about having relatives in these woods. He-Man didn't dare try to free his sword—doing so would endanger his friends. But now he wondered if there might be another way out of this situation.

First, though, he had to stall. He-Man sighed, as if he were preparing to divulge the great secret.

Skeletor was growing excited. "Yes, yes," he said, "tell me where to find the castle. Whisper it in my ear."

"You don't even have an ear!" Man-at-Arms called out.

"Details!" Skeletor scoffed, waving the bony fingers of his left hand in the air. "Whisper it in the general direction of my ear, then." He pointed with one of his skeletal fingers. "Right into this little bony cavity here. Tell me where you've hidden Grayskull so that I might obliterate your new home from the universe."

Tilting his head back, He-Man noticed two of the branches of the great tree growing thicker overhead. The bark was peeling back, revealing what looked almost like a face. Not a human face, exactly, but an older version of Kreannot. Skeletor's words resounded in his head. His new home? Adam didn't think of Castle Grayskull that way, even if they were staying there for now. Unlike Krass, he didn't think of the jungle of the Tiger Tribe as his true home, either. Nor did the palace feel right, even though he'd spent the first six years of his life there.

Maybe it was the Sword of Power. Maybe it was his strange new muscles or the force of the Grayskull energy pulsing through him. Or maybe it was something that had been inside him all along, but Adam was beginning to feel that none of these places in particular were his home. They all were, and it was his job to protect them all—including this mysterious grove.

The red-eyed, Havoc-infused, skeletal terror before him didn't understand that and never would.

He-Man hoped he was right about the tree at his back, and that it was listening. "Grayskull isn't my home," He-Man declared, "and I will not let you rule Eternia."

Now he really could feel the tree moving behind him. He spotted

139

the branches growing thicker, faster. Trap Jaw and Beast Man noticed, too.

"Ummm, Skeletor?" Beast Man started. "We have a little—"

"Quiet, Carrion Breath!" Skeletor snapped. "As for you, He-Man, you seem to have forgotten that this is the Age of Skeletor! I already do rule Eternia, and I answer to no one! I will not take care of this paltry planet. The planet will take care of me. Every living thing on Eternia will be my servant!"

"That's no way to lead, Skeletor," He-Man answered, "and I think you have the wrong idea about home." He glanced over at Battle Cat and Ram Ma'am. "Home is different for everyone. For some, it's a tribe in the jungle."

"Blah, blah, blah," Skeletor whined, mocking him.

"As for me? Well, you were wrong, Skeletor," He-Man continued. "My home isn't Grayskull. My home is *all* of Eternia"— now he raised his voice to a roar—"and I'll do whatever I can to protect it!"

These last words were like a bolt of life-giving lightning to the gigantic tree. A branch swung down from above and slammed against Skeletor's side. The Dark Master of Havoc dropped his staff, breaking its hold over both He-Man and Kreannot. The green chains of Havoc faded.

The hero dropped to his feet. Luckily, the distraction had given his friends a chance to escape as well: Man-at-Arms snatched the Power Mace from Trap Jaw's grip, and Kreannot was already regaining his strength. The legendary Moss Man stretched his treelike limbs wide and let out a deep, rumbling roar. He leaped to He-Man's side, facing Skeletor, Trap Jaw, Beast Man, and the phalanx of mind-controlled Red Legion guards. The giant champion clutched the Sword of Power and roared, "I'm no little prince, Skeletor. I am He-Man, and we are . . ."

"THE MASTERS OF THE UNIVERSE!"

Cowering, the dark prince of Havoc muttered, "Uh-oh."

As Skeletor lunged for his staff, Trap Jaw, Beast Man, and the suddenly terrified guards sprinted for cover, leaving the Dark Master of Havoc all alone. He-Man gripped the sword in his right hand and raised it high above his head, pointing toward the sky. The sigils of his power glowed as he yelled, "LIGHTNING STRIKE!"

The canopy of trees parted. Golden-yellow fireballs of Grayskull energy streamed down from the heavens like asteroids. He-Man soared up off the forest floor to meet them. The streaking spheres of pure energy struck him all at once, transferring their energy to the hero. The supercharged champion, now radiating golden light like some kind of human-shaped sun, dropped back to the ground. He jammed the tip of his blade into the soil and charged forward. Finally, he swung the Sword of Power up and over his head, sending forth enough bolts of Grayskull lightning to demolish a castle.

The power of He-Man's Master Strike blasted Skeletor up through the canopy of trees and into the night sky.

For a moment, no one moved or made a noise.

Trap Jaw and Beast Man turned their heads, listening.

The Havoc-brained soldiers paused, too.

Finally, after a five count, they all heard a loud crash as Skeletor landed in a distant field.

The lightning faded. His sigils stopped glowing. Yet He-Man wasn't finished. Clutching his sword, he turned to face Skeletor's minions. "Who's next?"

"I'll take Beast Man," Battle Cat growled.

Snarling, Beast Man raised his frightening whip, ready to fight, when a vine shot out from one of Kreannot's arms and grabbed the weapon out of his hands. More vines wrapped around the villain's furry orange legs and armored arms. He tried to swipe and scratch at the living chains with his sharpened claws, but he couldn't move.

"No fair!" Beast Man protested.

Trap Jaw hurried to help him. He raised the whirring, sparking laser chainsaw, ready to slice, when Battle Cat pounced on his back, smashing his half-metal head into the dirt. Behind the tiger, flashes of blue and yellow light flared. Battle Cat turned to see Man-at-Arms holding his Power Mace high, as the head of the weapon began to spin.

The madness of the fight all around him slowed almost to a stop as Man-at-Arms switched to Speed Build mode. He swung the Power Mace, smashing one of the Sky Sleds into its parts, grabbed two weapons from unsuspecting Red Legion guards, and rapidly combined the key components into something entirely new.

Meanwhile, He-Man turned to Rammy. "What do you say? Should we knock around some guards? Gently, of course." His friend stared up at him curiously for a moment. He knew that look. Something was bothering her. "What's wrong?"

Rammy shook her head. "Nothing," she insisted. He-Man could see she was lying, but she punched her open palm with her fist, refocusing. "Let's have a little fun," she suggested. She pointed to Kreannot. "Hey, Mossie, how tough are these trees?"

The creature still had Beast Man in the grip of his vines. "This grove is populated by some of the most ancient and powerful members of our tribe," he replied. "Nothing will knock them down.

Well . . . except a laser chainsaw," he added, noting the fallen trunk. "But thankfully that wasn't a Floranian."

Rammy looked up at He-Man. "Most knockdowns wins?"

"Deal."

The Master of Demolition shot forward like a missile. A blur of purple suddenly encircled the grove as Rammy bounced between the trees, knocking the hapless guards off their feet.

Within seconds, only a single soldier remained standing.

He-Man yanked the guard out of the way as Rammy approached.

"Thanks?" the soldier said, confused.

The champion crushed the man's weapon with his bare hand, then tossed him—a little harder than he'd planned—into a distant bush. The armored guard groaned and, despite the Havoc flooding his brain, didn't get up to fight back.

A breathless Rammy stopped. "Eleven. You?"

He-Man grimaced. "One."

Ram Ma'am laughed, but the fight wasn't over just yet. Beast Man had finally broken free of Kreannot's grip, and now he and Battle Cat were locked in a savage wrestling match. "Beast Man would like to see you and your friends in one of Rqazz's cages," the vile villain snapped.

Battle Cat roared loud enough to shake the trees. "You will never see me or one of my friends in one of your cages again!"

The huge tiger pinned Beast Man to the ground, but his rival quickly reversed the hold, flipping Battle Cat onto his back. He-Man was ready to race to his friend's side when a branch swung into place against his armored chest, holding him back. He looked over his shoulder to find Kreannot stomping forward. "Allow me," the creature intoned.

As Beast Man lifted one of his clawlike hands to strike Battle Cat, Kreannot swung a thick branch into his ribs. Skeletor's minion growled and rolled onto his side. Before Beast Man could climb to his feet, Battle Cat pounced. The tiger held one of Beast Man's arms. Kreannot held the other. Then Battle Cat lifted one of his Claws of the Wild. It glowed with power, and he looked as if he were going to destroy Beast Man for good. He raised the claw above his defeated foe and roared with so much force that Beast Man's orange-and-white face quivered. Then Battle Cat leaned in closer. "Run from this place as fast as your legs will carry you, Beast Man, or I'll ask my friend here to root you to this soil for eternity."

The broken Beast Man whimpered, agreeing to the deal, and Battle Cat moved cautiously away. Muttering something about how he used his arms to run, too, and not only his legs, Beast Man grabbed his cherished whip and rushed off into the darkness.

The glow of Rammy's destructive rampage had finally faded. She surveyed the bruised and battered guards and the surrounding trees. One of the enormous trunks looked slightly damaged. "You're sure they're okay, Kreannot?" she asked.

"No offense, friend," Kreannot replied, "but I doubt my fellow Floranians felt so much as a sting."

All that remained of Skeletor's squad now was Trap Jaw. He was backing up, severely outnumbered, and swinging his laser chainsaw from side to side. "I dare you to come at me," he growled, taunting them.

He-Man was thinking about accepting the challenge when Man-at-Arms sauntered casually across the clearing. He stood between his friends and his former mentor with his Power Mace swung up over his shoulder. "Are you sure about that, Trap Jaw?" he asked.

The brutal, blue-skinned Dark Master leaned forward. "Absolu—"

Trap Jaw cut himself off as a laser blaster the size of He-Man hovered into place above Man-at-Arms's head. Inside, a yellow light glowed brighter and brighter as the barrel of the weapon spun.

Trap Jaw's eyes widened. "What is *that*?"

"A little something I built out of the remains of a Sky Sled and a few rifles," Man-at-Arms replied with a shrug. "Want to see if it works?"

Instantly, Trap Jaw lowered his weapon.

The barrel of the genius inventor's creation kept spinning.

And Trap Jaw turned and raced after Beast Man as lasers blasted the ground in their wake.

Immediately, the trees overhead stirred as if a great wind was blowing through. Above the Masters, a flying vehicle broke through the canopy. Battered but not yet defeated, Skeletor hovered overhead on a massive roton. He-Man brandished the Sword of Power, eyeing the spinning base of the vehicle. The champion looked to his left, where Battle Cat and Ram Ma'am stood ready. On his right, Man-at-Arms and Kreannot glared up at the bony tyrant.

The roton pitched forward. Skeletor studied his opponents, then scanned the space. "Beastie?" Skeletor called out weakly. "Trap? Where is everyone?"

"They're gone, Skeletor," He-Man replied. "It's just you and the Masters of the Universe now. Your move, uncle."

The evil tyrant raised his staff slightly, as if he were going to strike, then swiftly spun his roton around and accelerated up and out of the forest. Over his shoulder, he called back, "Grayskull is doomed, you overgrown child! Doomed!"

24.

The Masters stood quietly for a moment. Man-at-Arms was the first to speak. "He didn't do his evil laugh."

"What?" Kreannot replied.

"Normally he follows his threats with a kind of cackle," Man-at-Arms explained. "It's oddly high-pitched."

"Yet intimidating," Battle Cat added.

He-Man tried to imitate Skeletor's devilish laugh, but his voice was way off. Man-at-Arms attempted to mimic it next, and Battle Cat wasn't even close. His cackle sounded more like a purr. Kreannot's version didn't resemble laughter so much as the sound of trees bending in the wind. The only one who didn't mock Skeletor was Ram Ma'am. He-Man nodded to her. "What about you?"

She smiled awkwardly, then shrugged. Her expression turned serious. "I'm not really in a joking mood," she admitted.

"What is it?" He-Man asked. "What's wrong? And what was Skeletor asking you about back there?"

"Nothing," she snapped. She kicked at a leaf on the ground. "Earlier, you said our jungle isn't your true home. You said all of Eternia is your home . . ."

"That's probably why my grandmother woke up," Kreannot replied, pointing back at the gigantic tree.

"So there *are* moss women," Man-at-Arms said. "Whoa. Cool."

"To be honest, we don't adhere to human conventions when it comes to gender," Kreannot replied.

"She doesn't look awake," Battle Cat noted. "She looks like a normal tree again. What did happen, anyway? He-Man, did you know the tree would help you?"

"I wasn't sure," He-Man said. "I was hoping so."

"She probably hasn't heard a human speak like that about Eternia for thousands of years, He-Man," explained Kreannot. "My relatives don't stir very often. I'm the only one who likes to run. What you said must have really resonated with her."

"Please thank her for us," He-Man replied, "and know that I meant every word of what I said."

"That's what I wanted to ask you," Ram Ma'am said. "You meant all that?"

"Of course, I did. Why?"

Rammy drew in a short breath, then stared back down at the ground.

"Adam?" Battle Cat interrupted.

Hearing his real name surprised him. He-Man turned to the tiger. "What is it?"

"I believe it's time for us to finish our task."

After they'd explained everything once more to Kreannot, he understood. "I'd be happy to provide several of my flowers," he said, "but they don't bloom on command. They only blossom when I'm happy."

"Aren't you happy now? We kind of just freed you from Skeletor. Plus, you're home!"

"This isn't my home. This is my birthplace. There's a difference. All the world is my home. I'm happiest when I'm roaming."

"So let's run," He-Man suggested.

"Run?"

"Roam, wander—whatever you want to call it. Let's start moving and see if we can get you blooming."

"I'm not much of a runner," Man-at-Arms admitted. "Would anyone mind if I followed by Sky Sled?"

None of them protested, and after Kreannot wished goodbye to his grandmother, the grove, and the still-rooted Floranians who lived there, the group started out of the forest. They began at an easy pace. The Masters weren't quite sure how fast the creature could move. As they emerged from the forest, though, Kreannot began to pick up his pace. His moss-covered legs moved faster and faster. Rammy wasn't one to lose a race, so she sprinted ahead, only to have Battle Cat soar past her, one great leap after another. Man-at-Arms cranked his Sky Sled up to full speed. He-Man was behind them all until he jumped nearly as high as the clouds, landing on the far side of the hill. The five of them continued racing over the next hill, and the next, until He-Man noticed a delicate pink and white flower blooming on Kreannot's chest. He said nothing at first, afraid that he might disrupt the process, but then a half-dozen flowers emerged fully grown. Seeing the growth, Man-at-Arms momentarily took his eyes off the moonlit landscape ahead of them. The inventor and his Sky Sled crashed through the tall grass in an overgrown field. Then he jumped to his feet and checked his vehicle. "We're fine!" he declared. He pointed to Kreannot. "And you're blooming!"

The Floranian's odd face formed a beaming wooden smile. Carefully, he plucked five flowers, one by one, and passed them to He-Man.

"Man-at-Arms," Battle Cat said, "are you ready?"

The inventor pulled a small device off the side of his Sky Sled, flipped open its glass lid, and dropped the flowers inside. Then he sealed the lid, quickly typed in a command, set the gadget on the ground, and stood back.

He-Man noticed that his friend was biting his lip. "You look nervous. Are you sure this is going to work?"

Man-at-Arms shrugged. "I don't know. I mean, it should. The science makes sense. But I've never attempted to replicate the molecular structure of a magical flower before."

"You humans are so very strange," Kreannot muttered.

While they waited, the Masters powered down into their normal selves. Kreannot remarked that he'd never seen anything quite so unusual in his four hundred years on the planet. The flash probably did look odd to an outsider, Adam realized. He was about to explain the whole Grayskull destiny story for their confused friend when Duncan's gadget began to glow.

The brightness intensified, then extinguished.

"Is it working?" Cringer pressed.

Duncan didn't answer. Then the gadget emitted a loud, old-fashioned ding that made him laugh. "I love that noise," he said. "Nothing like a fun little finishing touch, you know?"

"But did it work?" Adam asked.

"Whoa, whoa, whoa," Duncan replied, holding up his hands. "Patience, prince." He typed on the controls, then sat back and smiled. "This little gadget is sending instructions to all of our satellites, which will copy the scent and spread it everywhere."

"Simple," Krass said sarcastically.

"Exactly," Duncan replied. "A little science, some engineering—"

"—a dash of the Power of Grayskull," Adam added.

Duncan clapped his hands together. "And the world is back to normal!"

"How do we know if it's working, Dinky?" Krass asked.

Nervous, Duncan didn't answer. Adam glanced back at her. He was glad to see that she was engaged again. He'd have to ask her again later about that little sidebar with Skeletor. What had his uncle been talking about?

"Why don't we check that holo-globe of yours, Duncan?" Cringer suggested.

With a few quick adjustments to his electronic wrist gauntlet, Duncan switched on a holographic projection of the planet. A three-foot-tall digital model of Eternia rotated in the air above his arm. Kreannot gasped in wonder.

Adam proudly elbowed the Floranian. "Cool, right?"

"Astounding," Kreannot replied. "Wonderful magic."

"Not magic," Duncan said. "Technology. It just needs a few minutes . . ."

As they waited, Cringer redirected Adam's attention to several figures at the top of a nearby hill. There were only a couple of them at first, but as they scaled the rise, more appeared. The figures were dark and appeared to be covered in thick fur. It took Adam a moment to realize they were Pelleezeans.

"Those poor creatures," Kreannot said.

"A true tragedy," Cringer added.

"They need a home of their own," Duncan noted.

The engineer was right, and Adam wanted to help. But he wasn't sure how—it wasn't like He-Man could build them a village with a swing of his sword. Adam was watching the Pelleezeans, and puzzling over the problem, when Duncan grabbed his arm. "Look!" Duncan said.

The digital globe was brightening. The yellow clouds that had spread across so much of the planet began to thin into mere trails and wisps.

"It's working," Cringer said. "Fantastic, Duncan."

"It'll take a while until the mossflower scent spreads far enough," Duncan said, "but I think it'll actually work."

"Amazing," Kreannot said.

"He's pretty talented," Adam added.

"No, not him," Kreannot replied, gazing at the slowly spinning globe. "The planet. It's amazing! I didn't realize how many fantastic lands are still out there for me to explore!"

Cringer lifted a paw and pointed to the jungle home of the Tiger Tribe. "That's where my tribe lives."

Quietly, Krass stared at the spot.

"Yes," Kreannot said. "I remember! Beautiful country. Delightfully tasty water in the soil, too. But look at all these other lands! I had no idea there was so much more to see." The Floranian started bouncing with nervous, excited energy. He faced Adam. "Do you need me anymore?"

Adam looked to Duncan, Krass, and Cringer. He shrugged. "Now? No, I think we're all set."

"Wonderful," Kreannot replied. "I did enjoy meeting you all, but as I imagine you've noticed, I'm really only happy when I'm traveling. So, if you don't mind . . ."

"Go!" Cringer said with a laugh. "Go see the world."

Flashing a green-toothed smile, Kreannot raced off into the night.

Meanwhile, Krass was stuck on the holo-globe, her eyes focused on the jungle home of the Tiger Tribe. "Hey, Duncan, would you mind if I borrowed that Sky Sled? There's something I need to do."

"Sure," Duncan answered. "What is it?"

Adam glanced at Cringer. "If you're going back to the tribe, we could go with you—"

"No," Krass said. Her tone was firm, and Adam sensed there would be no talking her out of this decision. "This is something I have to do alone." The powered-down Master brushed her hair out of her eyes, opened her mouth as if she were going to say something, then turned and started back toward the hovercraft.

"Hey, Krass?" Adam called to her.

"Yes?"

"Be careful, okay? Tiger Tribe forever, right?"

She let out a short humph. "Sure, Adam. Whatever."

He watched as she climbed onto the Sky Sled and rose into the air. "I hope you find what you're looking for, Krass," Adam whispered.

The hovercraft grew smaller and smaller in the night sky. When it was no more than a speck, Adam, Cringer, and Duncan walked back to the edge of the forest, where the *Wind Raider* remained hidden. At the last second, Adam turned and noticed that the first bunch of Pelleezeans had been joined by dozens more, including a number of kids. Several motorized carts loaded with suitcases and boxes trailed behind them. They appeared to be traveling. On their way to search for a new home, he guessed. Adam had to find a way to help them, and those young Pelleezeans in particular. They deserved a home like everyone else. But where? Not the Ice Mountains—Granamyr had made it clear she wasn't fond of guests. Adam wasn't sure the Tiger Tribe would welcome them, either.

He stared back in the direction of the pirate port.

Duncan was a few steps into the woods, heading for the *Wind Raider.* "Aren't we going?" he called back.

Adam thought back to what they'd learned in Westwind. That mossflower-munching rogue had told them how the breeze there blew steadily out to sea. The wind could carry the Pelleezean odor along with it, ensuring they wouldn't stink up the town. Plus, Duncan had copied the mossflower's scent, and had the technology to reproduce it. "Hey, Duncan, can you make more of that mossflower aroma?"

The inventor returned to Adam's side. "Sure," he replied. "As much as you need."

"And you could build something that blows out the smell, too?"

"Yeah," Duncan said with a shrug. He swung his multi-tool

wrench up onto his shoulder. "I probably wouldn't even need to power up to get it done, either."

"Adam, what are you thinking?" Cringer asked.

"Well, I know we should be getting back to Grayskull, but before we do," he said, nodding at the figures in the distance, "I think we might be able to find a few other folks a new home."

25.

The girl and her desperate parents had made it halfway to the palace at Eternos when they noticed the yellow clouds of toxic air beginning to clear. The breeze now carried a flowery scent that reversed the devastation of the deadly perfume. They were walking down a dry dirt road, carrying most of their possessions, hoping that they might be able to find food and a place to live in the capital city, when her mother spotted the change. "Look!" she shouted.

The once-dying trees scattered along the roadside were changing color. Their leaves were enlivened as they turned from yellow to green. Flowers sprang up along the path, too, and the hills grew dense with grass, as if the season had changed from the darkest winter to the peak of spring in a mere instant. Another family passed them, hurrying back in the opposite direction. Each of them was smiling, and when the girl's father asked what was happening, the excited kids announced that the Masters of the Universe had saved them all.

The girl swung back toward her home first. Her parents suggested that they ought to be certain before returning, but she let them know that she *was* certain, and the determination in her step forced her parents to follow her lead. The return journey was faster—or at least it felt that way—and when the girl and her parents crossed over the last hill and spotted their farm in the distance, they were relieved to see that it had been restored to health. Once more, their crops were a bright, healthy green. The girl raced down the hill first and found her beloved daisies standing tall and looking as beautiful as ever.

Meanwhile, in the distant port city of Westwind, a crowd of Pelleezeans approached from the forest beyond. Several pirates rushed forward to stop them, blocking their way into town. They were led by a man in a battered tricorn hat. He was about to warn the skunk-like creatures to slink back to the woods when a drone hovered into view above them. An absolutely delightful and strangely familiar scent spread out from the miniature flying machine's fans, and the wind carried it past the pirate and through the streets and alleys of Westwind.

One of the Pelleezeans stepped forward and declared that she and her family were famished, inquiring about whether the pirate knew of any good places to eat. They were all voracious eaters, she explained, and to show that they could pay, the Pelleezean then flipped him a coin. A genuine smile spread across the pirate's face. He invited them all to dine at his restaurant and, if they wanted, to stay in Westwind as long as they liked. His only advice? Avoid eating at Eugenia's pub at any cost.

Thanks to He-Man and his friends, Eternia was quickly returning to normal. Yet it would be wrong to suggest that peace had come to the land. The Masters of the Universe had won this battle, safeguarding Castle Grayskull and its infinite power. But the Dark Master of Havoc would not be defeated so easily. The remaining piece of the Sigil of Hssss had yet to be secured, and Skeletor was back to brooding on the throne, plotting both his birthday party and his next devastating scheme to wreak Havoc on the universe.

The war for Eternia had only just begun.

ACKNOWLEDGMENTS

Thank you to the entire team at Abrams, including Andrew Smith, for convincing me that I had the power, if only briefly; Howard Reeves, for steering, shaping, and agreeing to go on this adventure; Sara Sproull, for working ridiculously hard to make it happen in record time; plus the Mages of Marketing Borana Greku, Savannah Breckenridge, Hallie Patterson, Patricia McNamara O'Neill, and Kim Lauber. Additional thanks to the fantastic team at Mattel for their guided tours of Eternia and fantastic creative input, including Rowenna Otazu, Ryan Ferguson, Melanie Hill, and the Director of the Archive of Forbidden Knowledge, Rob David, who may actually be from Eternia. Plus Jen Carlson, Susannah and Andrew for having a wedding near a forest filled with magical moss, Tim and Finn Carver for showing us some tall trees and mystical mountains, Bigfoot, the 232 swim club, and my thoroughly awesome family.